Gracelynn's Genie

A ROMANCING THE SPIRIT NOVELLA

CB SAMET

~~Romancing the Spirit Series~~

cbsamet.com

© 2020 CB Samet

Cover Design by: Get Covers

Print ISBN: 978-1-950942-14-5

Praise for CB SAMET

Four-time award winning author

"This tale is funny, thoughtful, and goes a mile a minute and I had a blast reading it. Bet you will too."

— GIGI READS (BOOKBUB REVIEWER)

"Samet's prose vacillates skillfully between various registers, expressing sensuality, suspense, and humor, as needed."

— KIRKUS REVIEW (ON ROMANCING THE SPIRIT SERIES BOOKS 1-6)

A ROMANCING THE
SPIRIT NOVELLA

GRACELYNN'S GENIE

CB SAMET

One

"I wish for an adventure." Grace hung upside-down, muscles trembling, sweat sliding toward her hairline. Her abs burned.

"Are you sure, Darling? This is your third and final wish."

Grace twisted to face her ghost-genie, watching those penciled brows arch. "I know the score, Constance. It's time."

Constance rippled, translucent in a haze of blue smoke. Her voice was a deep baritone—although rouge covered her thick lips. "But your life is already an adventure, Darling." She protested as she waved a hazy hand through the air. "You travel the world on your medical expeditions—South America, Africa, Eastern Europe." Masculine eyebrows had been replaced by a thin, penciled line with a feminine arch. Her eyes were framed by impossibly long, dark eyelashes.

Grace frowned as she strained to curl her body. Perhaps her life had once been an adventure. Now, though, it felt like a hollow, endless search for ...

Something.

"Adventure, Constance. What can you find for me?" She didn't want her genie ghost talking her out of her request.

Ten years ago, Grace had bought a bronze lamp during a medical mission. Like Aladdin in the fairytale, she'd unwittingly unleashed what she'd at first thought to be a trapped genie from within—in the form of the deep-voiced, shimmering Constance. Over time, Grace had learned that Constance was actually a ghost who spent her spiritual existence pretending to be a genie. Because she was a ghost, few people could see or hear her.

Two of Grace's three wishes had been used. Those wishes had brought her some of the best and worst times of her life. They were cursed wishes.

Misleading to even call them wishes, Grace thought bitterly, but she'd put off using the final wish long enough.

"Adventure," Grace repeated, and Constance pouted.

"You don't want an adventure. You want something reckless. Just like the reckless behavior that keeps launching you head-first into dangerous countries to volunteer medical care."

"Adventurous *and* reckless," Grace grinned. "Yes, let's do that."

After grasping the bar above her, she released her feet with the press of a button. When her legs swung down, she began a series of intense pull-ups.

"You know—" Constance fidgeted with the decorative silver coins on her blue pantaloons "—there are people in *this* country who need medical care. You don't have to travel to third-world countries to find people in need."

"I tried a free clinic here," Grace countered, breathless from her pull-ups. "We were robbed. And then we were sued." She shook her head and strained to pull herself up for her tenth pull-up. "Who sues a free clinic? Only Americans." The clinic won the case, but the ordeal had been so draining, Grace closed the clinic anyway.

"Getting yourself killed won't bring Daniel back," Constance murmured.

Although the words were spoken softly, Grace felt like a knife had been driven into her back. She dropped to the floor and shook out her aching arms.

"I'm sorry, Darling," Constance frowned. "That was uncalled for."

"*Wish*," Grace demanded flatly as she walked over to the quadriceps machine. She sat and began her leg extensions.

"Okay, okay," Constance sighed. "When do you want to leave?"

"The sooner the better." She hadn't traveled in over a month and was starting to go stir crazy in her large, empty home. "I just need enough notice to give the pilot time to file a flight plan."

Wherever they were going, the local pilot could get her to a major airport.

Constance narrowed her thickly lashed eyes. "So ... somewhere remote?"

"You know I like remote."

Constance chewed the ends of her blue, flashy nails. "And dangerous?"

"I eat danger for breakfast," she quipped, feeling the strain in her legs from the machine.

"Something heroic?"

"That's optional. I'm not so much looking for fame and glory." Grace wanted something to take her mind off being alone—a state in which she perpetually kept herself.

"Don't I know it." Constance's lips drew down. "It's maddening. I've advised sultans and kings—I've *made* sultans and kings, elevated from mere paupers on the street. You could be sensational with me by your side, if only you changed your wish to, say—"

"*Adventure*, Constance," Grace snapped though with no malice in her voice. "Work your genie mojo."

"Fine." Constance huffed. Then, she brightened. "Oh, I may have just the thing brewing. Let me focus."

Grace narrowed her eyes at the ghost's glowing apparition. Constance schemed behind those rippling blue eyes, but Grace wasn't unduly concerned. Whatever the future held, her third and final wish couldn't put her through as much suffering as the first two wishes had.

WADE RAWLINGS HIT the hard ground with a thud, jarring every muscle in his body. Gasping, he coughed moist dirt out of his mouth. As he looked around at his surroundings, he took a shaky breath. A circular prison—a dirt pit in God-knows-where, Colombia, South America—enveloped him.

He'd been dragged past a row of similar pits before finally being dumped into this one. Did other people languish in the neighboring holes—and, if so, how long had they been there?

This was not how he'd envisioned the end of his trip to South America. He'd left the Amazon rainforest after taking amazing footage of the rich vegetation, wildlife, and forest fires. Beauty and devastation, yin and yang. His photos and videos were intended to raise awareness of the blaze back in the United States and to be used for fundraising efforts to stop the fires. As his trip had wound to an end, Wade had planned an add-on shoot in Neiva, Colombia.

He'd never made it there.

Somewhere between Bogotá and Neiva, the bus he'd been riding in had been hijacked. Wade's crew of two other men—locals he'd hired to help navigate the countryside—were killed instantly when they'd tried to resist. Wade hadn't made that mistake—but he'd still been beaten, tied, and finally dumped here ... in a pit.

Of particular interest was how the bus driver had simply driven away from the hijacking, unhurried after Wade and his hired help had been forced off the bus. Had the driver been paid to inform the Colombian guerrilla fighters whenever foreigners boarded his bus?

Deep in the pit, Wade curled his knees up and clutched his side, feeling the tender bruises. The abductors had knocked him to the ground and kicked him when he'd initially moved with too much hesitation.

Now, he had to wonder how long his captors would keep him. As long as it took them to realize he had no influential connections or wealth back in the States. Sure, his pack had contained expensive photography and filming equipment—but that had been the extent of his wealth. Wade was certain that when his kidnappers discovered he wasn't ransom-worthy, they'd simply let him rot in this dirt prison.

Above him, darkness descended. All around, the noises of the jungle filled the air. Despair ebbed into his bones.

GRACE'S athletic figure moved lithely as she worked her way through routines on each of her exercise machines. While the woman was physically fit enough for any conceivable adventure—up to and including climbing Kilimanjaro if she so desired—Constance questioned the fitness of Grace's mental health for the task ahead.

Since Daniel's death two years earlier, Grace had grown increasingly reckless about her own safety. She might have saved many lives as a physician, but each new mission came at high risk, putting her in peril. Grace's behavior wasn't promoting her own longevity.

But the woman's escalating recklessness was at least partly Constance's fault. The wishes she'd granted Grace weren't wishes in the truest sense of the word. Constance couldn't perform instantaneous magic, but she *could* follow a hypothetical course of action in her mind's eye and see the potential outcome.

She'd possessed the ability to see into the future ever since becoming a ghost, millennia ago, but the gift had limitations. For example, Constance couldn't foresee *all* the ramifications a course of action might set in motion, because numerous and multiplying external factors played into a person's future over time.

This time, though ...

"*Eureka!*" Constance exclaimed.

Grace blinked at her, stopping her countless repetitions on the monotonous machine at the sound of Constance's startling exclamation.

"Picture this," Constance spread her arms wide and jiggled her body, until the shining coins on her pantaloons jingled loudly, "the Colombian jungle."

Grace cocked her head to one side. "You've piqued my interest."

"There's an American man held captive there—an innocent man! The clock is ticking until his inevitable execution, but *you* can save him."

"Can I?" With skepticism in her eyes, Grace drew back.

Honestly, sometimes Constance felt her dramatic flair when entirely unappreciated. "Yes! I can guide you there. *We* can save him."

"What's involved?"

"Obviously the plane rides there. You'll have to land on a remote airstrip in a small plane—and have a quick turn-around time to get back to the plane before you lose your opportunity to leave. That means one or two nights in the jungle—tops."

Grace started a round of upper body presses as she seemed to consider Constance's proposal.

"It'll be too risky for the plane to sit there and wait for us. What if I parachute in instead? Then we could have a plane fly in for a scheduled pick-up?"

Constance strangled back her opposition to Grace jumping out of a plane. She wanted to help Grace, but would this trip be a step toward healing? Or just a short reprieve before her next downward spiral?

"That could work," she said hesitantly, biting her lip.

Oblivious to Constance's concerns, Grace finished her set and finally stood, scrubbing a towel across her face. "How much time do we have?"

A glimpse of hope flashed through Constance. Maybe Constance's scheming could help Grace turn her life around. Maybe saving someone was what Grace needed to save herself.

Two

Constance cringed as Grace jumped out of a perfectly functional airplane. The genie didn't want to think about the seemingly countless number of things that could go wrong during an attempted parachute descent into the teeming jungle below. She couldn't comprehend this thrill seeking behavior when life was such a fleeting, precious gift. And yet, to feel alive, she'd witnessed people engage in activity that threatened death.

As Grace plummeted through the air, she clutched the heavy pack she wore across her chest—backwards, so her chute could deploy behind her. Fortunately, there was no wind or rain to make this ludicrous risk-taking even more dangerous than it already was.

If something went wrong, Constance could do nothing to intervene—a big fat *nothing*. Her apparition couldn't catch anything other than a drift.

Constance tried to reassure herself as Grace soared through the air that the woman *had* been fully trained in the suicide—er, *art*—of parachuting. She'd packed her own parachute, and she'd jumped two dozen times previously ... and it hadn't killed her yet.

But those had been controlled jumps, over flat land, and in ideal conditions. Constance kept her nervous thoughts to herself, first and foremost because showing fear was unbecoming of a mystical being like herself. Secondly, because she didn't want to distract Grace as she sheared through nothing toward the looming jungle canopy below. And lastly, because the woman probably couldn't hear anything but the roaring wind right now.

At twenty-five hundred feet, Grace pulled her ripcord and the dark green silk deployed perfectly. The parachute billowed out and sharply slowed Grace's descent. Now, floating smoothly, she neared the jungle canopy. As she descended, she maneuvered away from the rocks and ravines beneath her—but that left the only other option for a landing: trees.

Grimacing, Constance squeezed one eye shut, not wanting to watch but unable to look away.

Grace tucked in her hands and feet as she speared through the treetops. She passed through the branches and boughs—and only when her parachute snagged on the tree limbs above her did her descent come to an abrupt stop.

She grunted in pain. "Ow! Whiplash."

"You've got bigger problems," Constance warned, floating down alongside her.

Following Constance's gaze downward, Grace gulped. "I'm a bit higher off the ground than I'd hoped for." She couldn't simply unhook her harness and drop to the jungle floor below—not at this height. At least, not without breaking a leg. Instead, she worked the heavy pack slung across her chest loose.

Removing the thick coils of rope that had been wrapped around it, she released the heavy pack. It plummeted down before falling on the floor of the jungle with a heavy thud.

Constance gasped. "Be gentle, you brute! My lamp is in that pack."

Free of the heavy pack, Grace had more mobility. She wriggled and maneuvered, swinging back and forth from the straps of her parachute.

"It's fine," she grunted. "There are clothes around it. The only things that probably broke were my MREs."

As she hung from the parachute, she looked up at the state of it. "I'm won't be able to keep the chute. It would take too long to untangle it."

Using the rope she'd grabbed, she tied herself to a tree, connecting the rope to her parachute harness and then looping it over a thick branch. Next, she unhooked her parachute from the harness, dropping free, only to be caught by the thick rope she'd secured. Face red with the strain, she began lowering herself down to the ground below.

When her feet were finally on solid ground, Grace wasted no time recoiling the rope and retrieving her backpack, which she slung over her shoulders the way it was meant to be worn.

At last, Constance breathed a sigh of relief.

"Ready?" Grace asked, as if they were about to take a walk in the park, not trek toward danger.

Constance gave Grace a disapproving once over. She

was dressed for the occasion, at least. Grace wore khaki pants with multiple pockets, sporting a pocketknife and a flashlight. Her tank top left her shoulders and arms bare, and the skin shined with the coat of bug-spray she'd applied to avoid insect bites—and the diseases they carried.

Her blonde hair had originally been in a braid, but the leap from the plane and the death spiral toward the Earth had replaced that with a hairstyle that could only be described as 'dashingly wind-blown.'

Yes, Constance's plan might just work.

GRACE ADJUSTED her backpack as she hiked through the jungle, following the path Constance led her through. Exhilaration after the plane jump had her blood pumping and her feet moving swiftly.

Everything leading up to this moment had happened so quickly. The journey to the Colombian jungle had been condensed—a flight from upstate New York to JFK, followed by the flight from JFK to Bogotá, followed by renting a single-engine plane to drop her roughly ten miles from her intended destination.

Maybe if Constance had been a *real* genie, the trip could have been taken on a magic carpet, instead of airplanes and a parachute—but at least the travel time had enabled Grace to plan.

Grace needed enough food and water for two people for the extraction trip and had packed accordingly—plus she'd packed flashlights, flares, a lightweight tent, a blanket, meals-ready-to-eat, water filters, bug spray, netting, changes of clothing, and a compass. In addition to packing it, Grace had coated herself with so much bug-spray she imagined she'd probably glow in the dark.

That final item—the compass—Constance had been affronted by, because, in her opinion, Grace had her to serve as a ghostly guide and wouldn't need a compass. But 'always prepared' was Grace's motto.

On one of the connecting flights to Colombia, Grace and Constance had reviewed the layout of the camp where this American was being held prisoner. The genie had given Grace more details than a drone could have delivered.

Too bad Grace couldn't go to the authorities and ask them to extract the American prisoner; to do so, she'd have to explain that her inside information source was a ghost. Such a claim was unlikely to pass muster, even if such information could be used to prevent future kidnappings.

As she trekked, the quiet jungle hike reminded her of the time she'd once hiked the Appalachian trail—not long after Daniel's death. Nature and remoteness brought her comfort, and the labor of setting a brisk pace—not to mention the thirty-pound backpack on her shoulders— kept her from dwelling on her internal pain.

Constance floated ahead of her, a blue beacon out of place in a jungle ... then again, only Grace could see her.

"How much farther to the camp?" Grace asked, which was an entirely different question than 'are we there yet?'.

"In my prime, as Jinn Constantine to Memed II, who ruled the Ottoman Empire for thirty years and conquered Constantinople—I would have said two leagues. We called them *fersah*—but to you, I will say seven miles."

"You'll let me know of any danger?"

"I'll let you know about wires, mines, sentries, lions, tigers, and bears."

Grace snorted. "Does that make you the Tin Man?"

Her voice dropped a playful octave. "Darling, I'm the all-seeing Oz."

"Oh, begging your pardon," Grace quipped.

"If this doesn't go well, you've got bigger problems than flying monkeys."

She grunted her reply to Constance. The genie worried, but Grace had faith in her ability to find the path to safety in a tough spot.

The crunch of her boots on the path beneath her and the clamoring of the birds and squirrels distracted her from the danger lurking around her.

"See those green and red flowers?" Grace pointed toward petals that were vibrant with a waxy sheen. "Those are heliconia species."

They walked past Colombian oaks, Pekea-nut trees, and the Yopo tree with its fern-like leaves. The view was lovely, and the temperature wasn't unbearably steamy, either—although the humidity caused her to sweat straight through her shirt. She'd opted for long pants made of ninety-seven percent nylon, because they were protective, breathable, lightweight, and fast drying.

Although she enjoyed the hike, she hoped it wouldn't rain. Rain would soak her pack and add even more weight to it. That weight, and the rain-slick ground, would slow down the entire rescue trip. Because it was September, the rainy season was supposed to still be a few weeks away—but that didn't mean Grace wouldn't get wet.

In front of her, a yellow frog hopped from one emerald-colored leaf of an Aphelandra to another.

"Cute little thing," Grace noted, knowing full well that one kept one's hands to oneself around wildlife in foreign territory.

Constance floated in front of Grace, looking like she thought the jungle might come alive and swallow them both. "The golden poisonous frog," she breathed reverently. "That 'cute little thing' has enough poison to kill a dozen people."

"Oh!" Grace's eyes widened. "Is that the frog that native tribes use to make their poison darts?"

Constance swatted uselessly at a spiderweb, her hand passing right through it. "I don't share your enthusiasm—but, yes. Darts and arrows. Tribesmen hold the frogs over a fire and collect the toxins sweated from their skin."

"Well, let's not upset any indigenous tribes, shall we?"

Constance shot her a look over her shoulder as her lips twitched. "No raiding sacred temples, then."

Grace chuckled. "Look at you with your pop-culture references. I think that Indiana Jones scene was actually set in the Peruvian jungle—but, hey, that's not too far from here."

Grace continued her hike—step by step, hour by hour. She and Constance lapsed into comfortable silence, and Grace sensed—by Constance's escalating nervousness—that stealth was becoming paramount.

An hour before nightfall, Grace found herself a tree large enough to call home for the night.

After pulling on gloves, she made the arduous climb into the boughs of the towering tree. Once secure, she pulled her pack up after her, into the tree, and tied it off. Then, she tied off her rope to her harness—the same one she'd worn when she parachuted out of the plane that same morning. Next, she secured her hammock, stretching it across the space between two opposing branches. Finally, she draped mosquito netting over the hammock.

After grabbing water and a protein bar from her pack, she crawled inside her nest and pulled the mosquito netting closed behind her. Looking down at the jungle below, Grace surveyed the scene. At twenty feet above the ground, with foliage between her and the jungle floor beneath, she wouldn't be impossible to spot from the ground, but someone passing by in the dark probably wouldn't notice her.

Up in the tree, she was reminded of when she and Daniel had once gone zip-lining in Costa Rica. She'd been in medical school, and Daniel had been a practicing internist at the time. They'd been married for only a year at that point, and their love of travel had been one commonality that had brought them together in the first place—that, and a foolish wish.

She settled into the hammock, the netting whispering shut around her. The jungle murmured all around her, alive and indifferent. Her weary muscles tugged her tired body. Tomorrow, she'd attempt something she'd never tried before—a rescue mission.

Miles away, a man waited in a hole.

Sleep beckoned her, but she fought it long enough to whisper, "Hold on."

Whether she meant the stranger ... or herself ... she wasn't entirely sure.

Three

Hovering in the canopy of foliage, Constance watched over Grace as she slept—as she'd done during the physician's many dangerous trips, and as she'd done for sultans, kings, and queens over the centuries.

Perhaps time and experience should have made Constance a formidable advisor, but the longer she "granted wishes"—peering into the future and picking a course of action which would make a person's wish come true—the less certain she became that she could accurately fulfill such wishes. While Constance had once heralded herself as a mighty jinn—twisting fate and turning the tides of war—her actions after the ebb and flow of centuries seemed a meddlesome sort of arrogance.

Following a dormant eighty-five years, Constance's lamp was discovered by the young and carefree Grace—a refreshing woman, full of life. She and Grace had become fast friends, and Grace, who'd been content to be enamored by having a genie in a lamp, had let a full year pass before even asking for her first wish. And what a simple wish it had been. The college girl had wanted love.

Constance had set her on the path to love, but also, unfortunately, heartbreak.

When the inhabitants of the jungle—birds, monkeys, frogs, and big bugs—began squawking their early morning ruckus, Constance brought her attention back to the present.

Grace stirred. Her long blonde hair had curled at the ends in the jungle humidity, and her oval face had lightly tanned overnight from yesterday's sun exposure. Bright green eyes flickered open, and she instantly looked at Constance's expression.

"Trouble?" Grace asked.

"No trouble, Darling."

Reassured, Grace stretched. The hammock swayed with her motions. She sat up carefully and brushed away the long bangs covering her forehead.

Within twenty minutes, she had everything packed away and repelled back down the tree. She coiled the rope back around her backpack, picked up the harness, and read-justed everything as she secured it around her.

"Is our timing still good?" Grace asked.

So efficient, so driven. So devoid of enjoyment.

Because now was not the time to mention any of this, Constance only nodded. "You can sneak a note to the captive when we get to the camp. Then, we'll come back an hour later when the rebels are away from camp. That's when we'll make the rescue."

"Okay. Let's go save a life." She started walking.

Constance followed with a frown. This last act would

fulfill Grace's three wishes, which meant Constance would be free to leave her. Except Constance had always been free to go, or free to stay.

The 'wish' limitation had been something of her own creation—a rule she'd put in place a long time ago to limit how much time she'd have to spend with people who might try to abuse her ability to see into the future.

So, even after this 'wish' was provided, Constance thought perhaps she'd stay with Grace just a little while longer. They were friends, after all—and Grace hadn't stabilized herself after losing Daniel.

But as disastrous as her first two wishes had been, Grace might be eager to be rid of Constance. Perhaps that's why she'd made this third and 'final' wish.

Grace had everything money could buy, but money couldn't buy happiness. Could adventure? Constance was taking a gamble that she could transform Grace's wish for adventure into something more. Constance was, after all, a self-professed meddlesome genie—and she couldn't change her nature any more than she could really grant wishes.

WADE'S STOMACH RUMBLED, and he licked his dry, cracked lips. He simultaneously longed for raindrops to fall on his face and whet his thirst—and for no rain at all. Rain would turn his dirt pit into a mud pit.

A faint shuffling noise above had him raising his eyes. From up above, he spotted someone peering down at him —someone with a flash of blonde bangs.

A woman?

As quickly as her face appeared, it disappeared again. Then, the lattice roof of his caged pit lifted, and a bag tumbled down toward him. Before it landed in the dirt, Wade grabbed and fumbled with it, barely catching it. Glancing back up, he saw no one so he opened the delivery. The bundle contained a canteen, a protein bar, a harness, and a note.

> *Eat, drink, and put on the harness. I'll be back to hoist you out in an hour. Be ready to run. —Grace*

Wade stared at the neat, compact handwriting. Someone knew he was here. Someone had a plan. His throat tightened. He almost called out—*Hey! Wait!*—but clamped his mouth shut. No point advertising that his miracle had arrived.

But how did anyone know where to find him? And who'd be footing the bill for rescuing a nobody photographer from deep in the Colombian jungle?

He could worry about that later. For now, Wade committed to being ready for when this mysterious cavalry returned. With gratitude, Wade followed the instructions on the note—quenching his thirst and satisfying his hunger.

When he finished, he reread the note.

Cavalry? Or just one person?

Grace.

Amazing Grace.

'*How precious did that grace appear.*'

Surely, an entire team of operatives was needed to successfully infiltrate this camp. The Colombian guerrillas were ruthless, and Wade had already witnessed how they had no reservations in using either the butt or the bullet-firing end of their AK-47s against anyone who stood against them.

In his lifetime, Wade had seen violence and death first-hand—but yesterday's killing had been especially cold-blooded and terrifying.

Maybe 'Grace' was a code name or team name. *Team Grace.*

It could be—except it wasn't a very fearsome team name.

Still, the lyrics of Amazing Grace—*'I once was lost, but now I'm found'*—gave him hope.

After strapping on the harness, Wade began stretching his arms and legs. He suspected he'd only get one chance at escape.

Be ready to run.

GRACE CROUCHED BEHIND A TREE. Of the six pits in front of her, only one was occupied. Having only one person to rescue increased her likelihood of success. Soon, the Colombian rebels would leave the camp to go on another raid, according to Constance, and then Grace would be ready for action.

The guerrillas' cabins were several hundred yards from the pits, and she wondered if that was by design so they didn't have to hear their captives screaming for help throughout the night. After trekking ten miles through the jungle, Grace knew screaming out here would be useless, but perhaps the guerillas' victims wouldn't realize that if they were in a pit, desperate for help.

She used the time to create a decoy escape trail—making deep footprints in the dirt and mud and snapping off shrub and fern branches, heading off in the opposite direction to the one she intended to lead her rescued prisoner. Her fake trail would misdirect the Colombians once they noticed their captive was missing. When they began their search, they'd hopefully be thrown off course.

Grace couldn't take credit for the clever plan. One additional advantage to befriending a ghost familiar with all forms of battle strategy—learned over the course of thousands of years—was that Constance could coach Grace through various techniques of self-preservation, including misdirection.

In the distance, the sound of diesel engines roared.

"It's time," Constance said.

The lions are leaving their den.

Grace looped her rope around the tree nearest the pits before tossing aside the lattice roof of the makeshift prison. She lowered the other end of the rope—the one with the carabiner—down into the prisoner's pit.

After pulling on her leather gloves, she heaved the rope toward her, hand over hand, one after the other. Something heavy weighed on the other end of the rope, which she assumed to be the kidnapped photographer. All those repetitions in her exercise room paid off. Grace hefted up the heavy man, and when she felt the weight on the rope finally slacken, she peered at the edge of the pit and saw him pulling himself up and over.

Releasing the rope, she shook out the burning muscles of her arms as she strode forward and grabbed the man by the harness. She pulled until his entire body was free and away from the pit the rest of the way out, pulling on his harness until he was finally free.

As soon as he was on his feet, he stripped out of the harness and wrapped the rope up for storage, not saying a word. Grace watched, trying to get a measure of him. He wore mud-plastered khaki pants and a light blue button shirt rolled up at the sleeves. His wavy black hair matched a pair of intense dark blue eyes and three-days of accumulated stubble.

She swallowed. Even half-covered in dirt, the prisoner looked good—*and* he was clearly cool under pressure. She gave a narrow-eyed glare at Constance, who'd apparently neglected to mention that the man she'd led Grace to rescue was almost exactly Grace's age, very attractive, and ... *not* wearing a wedding ring.

Constance, hovering just over the man's shoulder, gave Grace a sheepish grin.

Irritation flashing through her, Grace turned, scooped her pack off the ground, and slung it back over her shoulders. This was meant to be an adventure—not a matchmaking service. A mission. Not speed dating with AK47s in the background.

Well, Grace could ensure it *only* remained adventurous.

"This way," she barked, heading north.

The man dutifully followed her. "Thank you," he called after her, still carrying the harness and rope. He kept effortless pace with her, despite Grace's fast stride. "I'm Wade Rawlings."

"Gracelynn Kowalski," she responded curtly. "And don't thank me yet. We're not out of danger—not until we're on the getaway plane."

"We have a getaway plane?" The awe in his voice was palpable, but did nothing to soften her mood.

"Yes."

"Is it just you?"

"Me—and my genie."

The genie she wanted to chastise, but now wasn't the time.

"Is that a metaphor for something? Like... inner compass, gut instinct?"

"Nope."

Grace could sense Wade's confusion, but she didn't pause or turn around to look at him. She continued the hike, keeping a brisk pace.

"How'd you find me?" he asked.

"Spiritual guidance. With attitude." She could certainly derail Constance's scheming if Wade thought she was crazy. But he wouldn't be interested in her anyway. She was broken, and he probably had a girlfriend.

"How did you find me so soon?" he asked, tone mild as though unruffled by her curt behavior. "I didn't think we'd even be reported missing yet."

We?

Crap. Had she left someone behind? For a second, Grace's mind returned to what she'd thought earlier—*he probably had a girlfriend.*

But then, with a stab of guilt, she remembered his crew.

Constance had told Grace that Wade's crew hadn't survived.

"I'm sorry about your team," Grace stammered. "Also, all of your equipment was in the main camp. I wasn't about to risk rescuing it."

His cameras, data, and video footage were all irretrievable.

"I'm just grateful you got me out."

"Don't—"

"—thank you until we're in flight. Yes, got it."

Despite herself, Grace grinned—but fortunately, with her back to him, he couldn't see it.

"So, you were getting footage of the Amazon rainforest?" she asked.

"The rainforest is being devastated by forest fires." Wade's breath deepened as he kept pace with her. "Over thirteen hundred square miles have been destroyed this year. I've been in South America for a month taking photos and video of the wildlife, as well as of the fires. My work was supposed to be used to promote save-the-rainforest efforts in the States."

Grace asked, "Is anything being done about the fires now?"

"Some money is being thrown at it, but not enough." Wade pushed aside a low-hanging branch. "Did Dixon send you?"

"Dixon? I don't know who that is."

"National Geographic," Wade replied. "He fronted me some money for the trip, in exchange for photos. He's the only one I know with the funds and connections to pull off a rescue, not that I'm complaining." He paused before asking, "So, is this something you do? Rescue hostages?"

"You're my first." She wouldn't explain that rescuing him was intended as a distraction from her own pitiful life. "I'm a physician. I usually do medical missions. This is ... a side project." Her voice held false cheer as she shot a menacing look at Constance—the traitorous genie who'd put her in a jungle with a handsome man with a good heart. With her back to her as she floated ahead, Constance missed Grace's glare.

"Like Doctors Without Borders? I did a shoot with them once."

"Yes, like that."

"Dr. Kowalski," he said, as if testing out the sound of the name.

"Just Grace is fine."

"So, do you have a clinic somewhere in Colombia, Grace?" The way he'd said her name sent shuttering delight along her spine—a foreign sensation she hadn't experienced in ages.

Stopping, she turned and finally looked at him.

Wade came to an abrupt halt, almost running into her because he'd been watching his foot placement instead of where he was going—or, maybe, he was too busy asking questions to focus on his surroundings.

She peered up at him, trying to get her bearings with his body close to hers. "No clinic here, Wade," she said coolly. "A spirit friend told me how to rescue you, so I did."

For a heartbeat, only the sounds of the jungle swirled around them.

Four

Wade blinked down at Grace. Her loose blonde hair was frayed at the ends. A pair of dark, green eyes—partially obscured by her chunky bangs—stared back at him. She had full lips and a slender neck. Her tank top exposed fit biceps, glistening with sweat, and the neckline revealed the swell of her bosom. He kept his eyes up though, out of respect. This woman was compact, agile, and not overly muscular—but she'd still probably give him a run for his money in an arm-wrestling match ... or dropkick him if she caught him ogling her.

"Spirit friend?" He raised an eyebrow. "Are you on some type of spiritual journey?"

"I suppose I am." After cocking her head to one side, she spun away and resumed walking.

He admired her backside as she walked ahead of him—at least, until he tripped on a root and barely caught himself before falling. Brave, formidable, and gorgeous.

Too bad she's crazy, he thought.

But if crazy got him out of this jungle, he would graciously accept it.

"Does your spirit friend have a name?" he asked, curious how deep the crazy ran.

"Constance."

"Can you see her? How does she guide you?"

Grace glanced back at him, as though puzzled by his line of questioning.

He was used to receiving that look. In fact, Wade's sister had always accused him of asking too many questions. Told him he should've been a reporter rather than a photographer.

"I can see her *and* hear her," Grace eventually answered. "I read somewhere that less than one percent of the population can see and/or hear ghosts."

Where did she read that? The National Inquirer? Wade wondered.

"Is she here now?" he asked.

"Yes, I'm following her back to the rendezvous site."

"What does she look like?"

"A transgender genie in a blue silk jumpsuit."

"Oh." His eyes widened. "That's fairly specific. Does she pop out of a lamp?"

"Sort of," Grace nodded with her back to him. "Spirits can be tied to physical objects if those objects held significance to them during their life. While Constance is anchored to her lamp, she doesn't poof out of it, or live inside it."

Again, Wade thought, *oddly specific.*

Perhaps under any other circumstances, the conversation would have been disturbing—the woman saving him talking about seeing and hearing a ghost, and all—but as they fled through the jungle, the strange topic helped distract Wade from his fear and fatigue.

"How long has she been a spirit?"

"Before Christ."

"Wow. I bet she's handy in Trivial Pursuit."

Grace paused, looked back at him, and finally laughed. She'd been so serious up until this moment that the unexpected laugh made him smile. He liked the musical sound and the way her entire face softened when she was amused.

"How long have you known her?"

Continuing onward, Grace moved a branch aside for him. "Ten years now."

"Oh! So, not a brief spiritual encounter then?"

"No—we're good friends. Perhaps *too* good of friends."

Because the comment didn't seem directed him, Wade didn't ask her to elaborate. Instead, he asked playfully, "You called her a genie. Does she grant wishes?"

Grace's shoulders tightened. "She grants trouble." She continued to press forward, her demeanor returning to the iciness of earlier.

Had his tone or his words set her off?

In a detached, clinical tone, she said, "We're going to be hiking until dusk. You might want to save your energy."

By not talking?

Wade didn't consider conversation an energy expenditure. He'd heard introverts did, though. Perhaps Grace was an introvert who'd rather speak to an imaginary genie than a real person. None of his business—except, he wanted to know more.

~

JUAN LANDA STARED at the empty pit. Around him, his men took off into the jungle, following tracks left by the man who was supposed to still be in the hole below him.

Impossible!

No one could climb out of the pits.

Based on a second set of smaller footprints, the American had help. But how was that possible? No outsiders knew about this camp. Even satellites couldn't spot it through the dense foliage.

Perhaps a heat signature drone could, Juan mused—but who had the money for one of those? Nobody who cared enough to find their camp, hidden within half a million square kilometers of jungle. Had the photographer been wearing a tracking device?

If a military force had infiltrated, they would have destroyed the camp and not simply rescued a single captive. Besides, how could a rescue team have arrived so fast? Had someone witnessed the kidnapping? That would be the only explanation.

"*Culicagado,*" Juan swore.

He *needed* that American—and whatever ransom he was worth. Everyone had someone willing to pay for his or her life.

Juan allocated his money to a worthy cause. His outfit was one of five guerrilla cells in the jungle, each working off the grid to save money for the coming revolution. Colombia's puppet government needed to be replaced by patriots. Because of greedy politicians who cared more about their suits than their people, foreign businesses were stripping the country of its resources—resources that needed to be nationalized for the sake of Colombia's indigenous people.

Juan's phone rang. He snatched it from his pocket. "Hello?"

"I have a sweet proposition for you."

"I'm a little preoccupied, Sal."

"Too busy for a rich American?"

I lost my last one, Juan thought.

Unless his *compatriota*, Sal, referred to the one he'd just lost.

"I'm listening."

"An American woman—a physician—parachuted out of my plane yesterday. I'm supposed to pick her up tomorrow at one of the landing sites."

Juan raised an eyebrow. "Why was she parachuting into the jungle?"

A lone American parachuted into the depths of the Colombian jungle? At the exact moment Juan held another in captivity?

These events were too coincidental for him to dismiss.

"She said she wanted to go sightseeing," Sal grunted. "Anyway—she's a doctor, *and* she had enough money to rent my plane solo. I figure she'd be worth twice my usual fee."

Juan lit a cigarette and took a drag. Phone clasped to his ear, he walked back to his tent. This American woman would be worth twice Sal's fee—*if* Juan captured both her *and* the man who'd escaped.

"Okay," Juan agreed, "but you only get paid when we have her in custody."

"No, I get a finder's fee."

Juan flicked cigarette ash onto the ground as he looked around his tent. He couldn't put together that much cash fast, so he'd have to have something valuable to offer the pilot instead.

His gaze landed on the pile of cameras and video equipment they'd confiscated from the photographer. Probably worth a few thousand American dollars—and the pilot could sell it in any major city.

"Okay," Juan growled. "I'll bring you a finder's fee. Which landing site?"

"*Serpiente verde.*"

"What time do I need to be there tomorrow?" Juan would continue his search for the photographer with his soldiers, right up until the rendezvous time. If his men found the man *and* the woman first, Juan wouldn't have to pay Sal anything.

Five

Constance glided through the air as Grace and Wade slogged through the jungle in silence. The infuriating woman wasn't even trying to be friendly—and Constance knew Grace was fully capable of amicable behavior. She'd had forged many friendships during her medical missions.

Today, though, the exasperating woman seemed to be deliberately thwarting the development of any kind of friendship with the man she'd rescued—perhaps because she suspected Constance of attempting to matchmake the two of them... which, in her defense, Constance *was*.

But Grace needn't be so stubborn about it!

In any event, saving Wade's life should go a long way toward counterbalancing her 'crazy talk' about conversing with ghosts.

Grace almost never talked about seeing ghosts. Today, she wouldn't shut up about it.

Constance knew why. The more unhinged Grace

sounded, the farther this handsome photographer would stay from her heart.

"You could ask questions about him," Constance prompted. "Maybe seem interested?"

"I'm not," Grace snapped back.

"Not what?" Wade asked. Because he couldn't see Constance, he'd naturally assumed the comment had been directed at him.

Grace corrected herself. "I'm not, um, sure the weather is going to cooperate. Feels like rain."

Feels like rain?

Constance looked up at the sky.

Oh, my!

It *was* going to rain, and a downpour would have a disastrous impact on their ability to reach the rendezvous point by tomorrow afternoon. Constance began exploring different possible outcomes, focusing her ability to see into the future.

One truth soon became apparent: If Grace and Wade were going to survive, they'd have to take a detour—and Grace wouldn't like it.

GLIDING IN FRONT OF GRACE, Constance took a sharp, southbound turn. Grace followed Constance, and Wade followed her.

"You're right about the rain," the ghost explained. "We need to make a detour."

"How do you keep your bearings in this place?" Wade asked. "The canopy is so thick. I can't even tell what time of day it is." He raised his bare wrist. "Plus, they stole my watch."

"I'm following the ghost," Grace replied curtly, feeling a little guilty that he was forced to put all his trust in her while she projected her frustration with Constance toward him. If she wasn't deliberately undermining Constance's efforts at matchmaking, Grace would have had the decency to lie and comfort him.

Wade cleared his throat. "So, you're telling me that my entire fate—from you finding me in that pit in the first place, to us reaching the plane to escape—relies on the help of a ghost named Constance?"

"She prefers to be called a genie—or jinn, or ginnaye," Grace corrected him. "Besides, she's gotten me this far. I've done ten medical missions—and avoided capture or death three times."

He scoffed, but somehow the sound of disbelief was more humor than irritation. "I've been in and out of war zones taking photographs, and avoided a similar fate more times than that, but I've never claimed spirits were involved."

In and out of war zones? Risking his life? Grace took a moment to absorb that tidbit. Constance had told Grace that Wade had been in more than one tight spot before, so he wouldn't be in pieces when she pulled him from the pit.

"What was your third wish?" Wade asked, changing the subject.

She stopped, and for a moment the jungle sounds seemed louder than his voice. Turning slightly, she cast soft words over her shoulder. "You've heard the saying '*be careful what you wish for*'? Well, it's true."

"Grace—"

She turned back and continued walking, not letting Wade finish his sentence.

That would be the end of it, she was sure. The photographer, who risked his life for impactful images to change the world, had now seen her spirits—*and* seen her broken. There'd be no burgeoning friendship between them, and Constance's matchmaking efforts would fizzle into oblivion —where they belonged.

Raindrops began to fall, tapping out a gentle melody on the canopy of trees.

"Should we set up something to collect rainwater for drinking later?" Wade asked.

"I've got a Life Straw filter," Grace called back. "It'll remove bacteria and protozoa from any water source and make it drinkable. But I don't want to stop until dusk."

"Can I at least carry something? I've only got the harness and rope. You've got all the weight in your pack."

Constance turned her head, floated in front of Grace, and scowled. "Let him carry something. It can't be any heavier than the mound of misery you insist on carrying with you wherever you go."

Grace rolled her eyes and replied to both of them by snapping, "When we stop for camp for the night, we'll sort out how to divide it up. No stopping before then—we don't have time."

Constance's words wriggled under Grace's skin, though.

The misery you insist on carrying.

Choosing to cling to her grief was voluntary. Grace knew that, even if hearing it was hard. Daniel had been gone for two years now, and Grace still hadn't let it go. She would never let the emotions go—but she knew she didn't have to wear them like a shield, or like shackles. Daniel wouldn't have wanted that anyway.

"I bet the kids love you on road trips," Wade said as he followed her through the dense jungle, oblivious to her inner turmoil. "Do you allow bathroom breaks?"

"They have to pee in a cup," Grace said—and then, sensing his shock, reluctantly added, "I'm kidding. I don't have any children. You?"

"No children," Wade replied. "I was married once, but she decided she didn't like my working environment. Said she felt like she'd married a soldier—one who may or may not return from each tour of duty." He sighed. "I'm mostly to blame, I guess. I didn't make enough effort, and we were both young."

Grace hadn't expected Wade to open up like that. She certainly hadn't planned on doing the same, but his sharing caused a nagging sense of obligation to well up inside her.

"My first marriage—also too young," Grace reluctantly offered, "ended when we discovered we were incompatible in all the nuances of life: hobbies, travel, money management, and even monogamy." She sighed. "The first ended badly. The second was amazing. He died in a bike accident …"

"That's terrible." His voice sounded thick and empathetic. "How long ago?"

"Two years."

Sometimes, the ache is still so raw it feels like two days.

"I guess spirits are safer relationships," Grace continued. "Maybe that's why I kept Constance around so long. She doesn't cheat, lie, or steal. And she can't die on me."

Constance glanced briefly back at her, eyes full of compassion.

Wade said, "But you're living your life, at least. I've seen a lot of people simply exist instead of living. You haven't shut out the world, despite your suffering."

"I became a physician to help people," Grace said quietly. "I have no intention of stopping that." She paused before asking, "Are you normally this positive and encouraging? Or only toward people who rescue you?"

"Probably mostly the rescue."

When she glanced back, Wade grinned at her. The rain had drawn his dark waves into curls, and drops of moisture ran down his cheeks. The drops had become a downpour.

"Water break?" he asked.

She stopped, unhooked the canteen, and handed it to him.

He took a long drink. "Do your parents know you venture into jungles and save complete strangers?"

"I always let them know which country I'm going to, and for how long—but they don't know the details." She chuckled. "Better for my dad's blood pressure that way. I'm sure they assumed this was another medical mission trip."

"Are you close to them?" He took another drink before handing the canteen back to her.

"We don't live close, but we talk every week. My parents live in Nashville." She reattached the canteen and took her own drink from the straw attached to the water pouch tucked into her backpack. From the side pocket, she pulled out a packet of trail mix and handed him the bag.

"Nashville? Is that where the name Gracelynn comes from?" He munched a handful of trail mix.

"Yes, actually. My dad is a huge Elvis fan. Apparently, if I'd been a boy, I would have been Elvis. He had to settle for Grace."

"I like Grace."

"Well, much to my mom's chagrin, my dad still calls me Elvis. Drives her crazy. Of course, that's probably part of the reason he calls me that."

Wade chuckled. "Well, you look much more like a Grace than an Elvis."

"Thank you. Thank you very much."

"Not a bad impersonation." He grinned, an expression that warmed something inside her.

Grace winked. "You should see me in my blue suede shoes."

Her face grew hot despite the cool raindrops. Was she actually flirting? In a jungle? With a man she barely knew?

Ugh—she must've come across as *so* lame. At least Constance was only eavesdropping and not adding her own commentary right now.

She needed to focus on the rescue. They'd escaped the camp and put distance between themselves and the rebels, but safety wasn't guaranteed until they were out of the country.

She didn't want her first rescue mission to be her last.

Six

W ade couldn't help but admire Grace's red cheeks, framed by the blonde hair clinging to the side of her face and neck. The unflappable jungle doctor on a mission blushed when she flirted, transforming the prickly front she'd put on initially. He appreciated the flirting, but it made him notice how her soaked shirt clung tightly to the curves of her athletic body.

He forced his eyes back to hers, saying, "The rain is probably a good thing. It'll wash away our tracks."

She nodded, adjusting her backpack.

"Here—I'll take it." He approached and began hoisting the heavy pack off her shoulders.

When she turned, her footing slipped in the mud. He tried to catch her, but his feet were swept out from under him as well. They both landed in a tangled heap, and their bodies began a rapid descent through the slick mud.

They were cascading down the jungle slopes, like they were riding a log flume, and all Wade could do was cling tighter to her to avoid being separated. A thick root nearly clotheslined them.

As they slid through the mud, Wade desperately wondered if he could angle his body in front of hers in order to absorb the brunt of their landing whenever it came.

Suddenly, the bottom fell out from beneath them, and they plummeted through the air. When Grace unleashed a panicked gasp, he realized that was the first sign of fear he'd seen or heard from her.

Looking down, a flash of shimmering sapphire greeted him seconds before water engulfed them. The river hit like a fist. Cold closed over his head.

He fought the heavy drag of his wet clothes, fumbling for the backpack. Grace's fingers were locked around one strap, knuckles white. Tugging the backpack close to him, he kicked hard, hauling them both upward with the pack keeping the two of them tethered.

As their heads broke the surface, he took a gasping breath. The fast-flowing river they'd plummeted into carried them swiftly north.

"There!" Wade cried, indicating a bank where they could both swim.

"It's on the wrong side of the river to get to the rendezvous point!" Grace shouted, splashing and spluttering. "And Constance says there's a coral snake in the tree by the edge!"

The icy chill that instantly shuddered through Wade had nothing to do with the temperature of the water. "Let's *not* go there!"

Snakes. He'd been so excited about escaping that he

hadn't been thinking about jungle snakes. What were the rules about stripes and danger?

Red touches black, no worries for Jack. Red touches yellow, dangerous fellow.

He mostly hoped he'd never get close enough to see red touching *anything*. He might not believe in ghosts and genies, but if one was warning him about snakes, then he would listen.

He and Grace swam toward the bank on the opposite side of the fast-flowing river. They struggled to pull themselves out of the water by clawing through the mud and tree roots. Eventually flopping onto the safety of the rain-soaked bank, they gasped desperately for breath.

After a moment to compose themselves, he struggled up—shaking out the sodden backpack. Beside him, Grace squeezed water out of the front of her shirt.

"You okay?" he asked.

"Shaken, not stirred," she snorted. "Dang. Now I want a martini."

As he pulled the backpack on, Wade winced, feeling a sharp pain in his side.

Her voice was filled with concern. "What is it?"

"Probably just bruising." He grunted. "The kidnappers had a little fun softening the toes of their boots on my ribs."

"Let me see." She leaned closer.

Although he liked her concern and the idea of her hand on him, he shook his head. "Let's just finish getting where we're going for the night." He might not be a physician, but even he knew not much could be done if he had broken ribs —not here in the jungle.

As they resumed walking, wet clothing and soaked

shoes weighed him down, but each step took them both closer to escaping the jungle.

After fifteen minutes, they finally pushed between fanning ferns and found themselves in a small clearing. The clouds overhead had parted, and sun streamed through the tree leaves. Light sparkled off the surface of a small waterfall cascading down onto a stone ledge before emptying into a shallow pond.

"Oh, Wade." Grace's voice filled with astonishment as she stared at the view. Then, she shook her head, as if listening to a voice he couldn't hear. "Right—thank you, Constance."

He looked at her, raising an eyebrow. "This seems like a good place to rest for the night."

"And to take a shower," Grace added, voice all eager anticipation..

Spinning in a slow circle, he gauged the clearing. A tent would fit nicely off to one side.

When he came back full circle, he discovered Grace tugging off her shirt, presenting her back to him.

"Whoa! What are you doing?"

She stopped and turned to look over her bare shoulder at him.

"I told you I was taking a shower—and then you turned around! I thought we were on the same page."

He averted his eyes. "Okay, okay—sorry. I didn't realize you meant *right* now." He turned his back to her, shrugged off the heavy backpack, and busied himself unloading the contents they needed.

When he finally had the inventory arranged, he peeled

off his wet socks, boots, and shirt, and grabbed the small bottle of soap he'd found in the backpack.

"Soap?" he offered.

"Yes—and there's a blanket in there we can use as a towel."

He side-stepped over to Grace, extending his hand to pass her the soap—and catching a glimpse of her bare, toned legs.

There was no place close to the waterfall to hang the blanket for her, so he stood there instead—blanket in hand, staring at a red *Passiflora* that bore vibrant, slender petals.

"Thanks." She lifted the blanket from his hand and walked past him, towel wrapped around her.

"My turn."

After peeling off his sodden pants, he carried them, along with his shirt and socks, to the waterfall. He left on his boxers—which, to his mind, was the equivalent of a swimsuit. He had no intention of clinging to modesty in the middle of a jungle.

He stepped beneath the cascading waterfall and closed his eyes—letting the water wash away the coat of mud on him. Then, he scrubbed dirt out of his hair and off the rest of his body. Finally, he washed his clothes, hanging them to dry on a marmalade bush.

Grace, now dressed again, handed him the blanket. For a second, he thought he'd caught her staring at his bare chest, and he felt heat in his cheeks as he dried off.

Now who's blushing, Wade?

When he finished, she handed him a wad of spare clothes with a toothbrush on top.

"You brought me a change of clothes?"

She shrugged. "When Constance told me you were being held at the bottom of a pit, I figured you'd want clean clothing."

He checked the tags. "You even got my size!"

"Courtesy of Constance," Grace nodded. "She mentioned a few things about you—" she shot an annoyed look to her right—as if to somebody Wade couldn't see "—and neglected to mention a few others."

He raised an eyebrow. "What other thing?"

"Never mind. We need to make camp."

"I thought that spot over there would make even ground for a tent."

Grace bit her lip, placing her hands on her hips. She gazed upward. "No. It might rain again, and this area is prone to flash floods. We need to camp up in the tree."

"*In* the tree?" Wade rubbed the back of his neck. "I've slept in some strange places, but never in a tree before. This'll be a first for me. Do we strap ourselves to the branches or something?"

More importantly—would there be snakes up there?

Grace stepped into the harness and pulled it on. "Not exactly."

Overhead, thunder rolled again. Somewhere in the distance, something howled.

Tonight they'd sleep in the trees. Tomorrow they'd find out if the jungle planned to let them leave.

CONSTANCE HOVERED near Grace while she set up the hammock. She used the tent as a tarp for a roof.

One hammock. Two people.

45

Events were progressing nicely.

"You were peeking as he showered, Darling."

"So were *you*," Grace fired back.

Constance chuckled. "Well, yes—who wouldn't admire those broad shoulders and muscular chest? Yum, yum."

"You know, he's *also* a renowned photographer—dedicated to bringing the world the truth in pictures."

Beneath them, Wade watched Grace work, but he was out of earshot. He couldn't safely join her in the tree yet, since Grace only had one harness.

"Yes," Constance murmured, high above him. "Well, the brains are the bonus to the brawn."

"Maybe the brawn is the bonus to the brains," Grace retorted.

Constance waved a hand in the air. "*Toe-may-toe, toe-mah-toe,*" she paused, "and you l*ike* him." She jabbed a finger at Grace.

She rolled her eyes, tying one end of the hammock off. "Of course I *like* him. He's smart, adventurous, good-natured, and—yes—attractive." Her eyes narrowed. "I find it interesting—and no coincidence, I'm sure—that you picked someone my age and *single* for me to rescue."

Constance beamed a smile. "You asked for an adventure. You know I never underdeliver."

"No, Constance, you certainly do not."

Constance frowned. The conversation had been focused nicely on Wade, and then she'd inadvertently reminded Grace of the wishes with that last statement.

"Can I do anything?" Wade called up to her.

"Open the MREs," Grace suggested. "We'll eat."

Grace turned back to Constance. "You realize we have a

logistical problem here, right? I brought one tent—which is now our roof and protection from getting rained on all night—and one hammock. That's now the only bed."

Constance grinned and batted her excessively long lashes. "I don't see that as a *problem*, Darling."

"One person can sleep in the hammock and the other strapped to the tree," Grace considered, "but I still only have one mosquito net."

Constance poked out her bottom lip as she clicked her nails together. "I can see only one logical solution."

"Of course you can." Grace finished securing the ties at the other end of the hammock.

"Remember to sleep on his right side. The hairline rib fractures are on the left."

Tonight, romance under the stars.

Tomorrow, flee from impending danger.

Seven

As Grace and Wade ate the food, sitting on a log beneath the hammock, they discussed their families. Grace was an only child, while Wade had an older sister. Grace lived in upstate New York, while Wade mostly lived wherever the next job took him. She enjoyed the casual exchange and how easily they conversed.

Chewing a spoonful of MRE, he asked, "How did you discover Constance?"

"Are you saying you're a believer now?" Grace playfully nudged him with her elbow.

"I'm saying some of the things you've known are uncannily accurate, so I don't know what to believe."

Grace nodded, feeling confident enough to speak about it. "I discovered her lamp while I was a medical student," she explained. "I bought it and took it home to my dorm room. When a genie seemingly popped out, I freaked out. Lucky for me, my dorm roommate could see ghosts, too— she explained to me how they work."

"How they work?"

"Some people see and hear them," Grace nodded. "Some only hear them. Some ghosts have a stronger presence than others. Some can see the future or glean information from people."

"And some grant wishes?"

Grace sighed. Wade wasn't going to forget about the wish thing.

Not that she minded. He seemed pleasant enough to talk with so far. Why not divulge her past to a stranger? It seemed fitting, as the sun set over them in the depths of this Colombian jungle.

"Not *real* wishes per se," Grace explained. "Since Constance can see the outcome of any set of intended actions, she can tell someone which course of action to take to achieve that '*wish*'."

"Like studying harder to pass an exam? Or like entering a particular set of numbers to win the lottery?"

"More like the latter."

Wade's brows shot up. "Wow. Okay, then—so what was your first wish?"

"Probably what half the twenty-two-year-old women of the world want. Love."

"You wished for love?" His tone was more awe than incredulous.

"I did—and Constance made it happen. I positioned myself in the right place and at the right time—for Mr. Wrong. He and I fell madly in love before actually *knowing* each other. It was all passion and no substance, and as simmering passion went as flat and stale as day-old champagne, we both discovered how little we had in common."

Grace took a drink of water. "Or rather, I found out

49

how dishonest he'd been about who he was—not that I was entirely truthful, either. I never mentioned Constance, for example." She sighed. "Anyway, the divorce proceeded with haste. Not painless, but quick. I was devastated at the time. Young and divorced, and so terribly naive."

"That's brutal. I take it Constance's predictions only go so far."

"Yeah. They're short-term predictions, since longer outcomes inherently rely on so many more variables."

"I'm guessing wish number two had nothing to do with love?"

Grace chuckled. "You are correct. I was twenty-four when I cast the second wish. I went for money this time. I was in medical school, living off Ramen noodles, and staring at a quarter of a million dollars in student loans."

Wade winced. "Lottery numbers?"

"That probably would have been smarter. Unfortunately, my request was a little vaguer. I just wished for money—and nothing shady about how it came to me. Constance led me to Daniel, and the true love I'd been looking for with my first wish."

Grace took a deep breath. "He was a practicing physician. Together, we lived frugally and paid off my loans. We were on a path to financial independence by the age forty-five. I'd thought that was the extent of it—wish granted. Two actually, because I had love back in my life."

She massaged her temples.

Wade placed a hand on her shoulder.

"I'm sorry, Grace. If it's too painful..."

Actually, it was the opposite. The more she talked, the more a weight lifted from her chest. "It's painful," she admitted, "but I think I'm past due for sharing. You're the first to hear the true story." Grace took another deep breath before explaining. "A car hit Daniel while he was out riding his bike. He died, and he left a trust fund. It's a fund I never knew he had, and he left it all to me. That—and a life insurance policy."

"What are you telling me?" Wade smiled gently. "That I'm eating dehydrated ice cream in the depths of the Colombian jungle with a beautiful millionaire?" His eyes twinkled. "One who just saved my life?"

Grace shrugged. "I guess. But I'd trade all of that money in a heartbeat if Daniel could just come back."

Wade swallowed.

"Anyway—" Grace ran her fingers through her hair "—that was two years ago. Two days ago, I made my final wish." She turned her head, and their eyes met. "I asked Constantine for an adventure, and here I am."

Wade smiled. "I'm grateful your adventure meant you came to my rescue."

"Ah." Grace gave a tsk. "You say that now." She scraped the last bit of MRE from the pouch, avoiding his gaze. "You may revoke your gratitude once you hear the sleeping arrangement."

WADE ADJUSTED his body as the sound of rain pattered on the tent above him. Grace lay beside him in the nylon hammock, her head resting on his shoulder.

"Are you comfortable?" he asked.

They'd tried side-by-side and back-to-back; in the end,

gravity had made the decision for them. This was the only way to fit two bodies in one hammock without someone ending up in the mud.

"Maybe too comfortable," Grace admitted. "My eyes won't stay open much longer—especially with the sound of the rain overhead." She shifted in the hammock—to the point that Wade wondered if she was inadvertently snuggling up to him. "Did you know you're incredibly warm? It's like you're my personal bedwarmer. I got chilly last night because this hammock doesn't hold any heat."

Wade smiled in the darkness.

Hmmm. The woman bold enough to launch a solo rescue mission in the guerrilla-infested Colombian jungle fell to nerves rambling in the arms of a man? He felt flattered.

He kept his voice low as he spoke. "You know, we all wish for things in life. Some come true and some don't. Bad things happen when we make mistakes, and bad things happen even when we don't. Sometimes, good things happen when we make mistakes." He let out a deep breath. "My point is—I hope you don't blame yourself, or your ghost, for every bad thing that's happened to you or the people you love. It sounds like you live life to its fullest extent, and that in and of itself is remarkable."

Grace's fingers found his in the dark, tentative at first, then settling as if they'd done this a hundred times.

He hesitated, feeling her pulse flutter against his palm. Darkness made people brave—or foolish. He lifted her hand and brushed his lips across her knuckles, a gentle press of warmth in the cool, damp air.

Her breath hitched. Then their joined hands relaxed

back onto his chest, right over the steady thump of his heart.

So, maybe she had money, and maybe she had a genie. Wade couldn't offer Grace anything spectacular, but it seemed that what she needed more than anything was comfort—that, he had an abundance to offer.

She let out a contented sigh as she relaxed into him. Soon, her breathing became slow and rhythmic.

As he listened to the steady fall of rain overhead, he pondered the complexities of this woman. He'd seen many things on his global travels, but nothing that would make him believe in ghosts. Until now.

He had no explanation for how someone with no military training could infiltrate a rebel cell in the depths of a foreign jungle—and rescue him just three days after his initial abduction. Those were impossible odds—unless you had a genie in your pocket.

He'd have to process all of this later. Tonight, he needed rest—and tomorrow, they needed to be at the rendezvous to meet that plane.

While he hoped the trouble was behind them, he wouldn't rest easy until he left the country behind.

JUAN'S wet and deflated men ambled back into camp empty-handed. They hadn't found the Americans. He and his team had until noon tomorrow to do so—otherwise, he'd have to pay that pilot and then seize the *gringos* from him.

Tonight, though, Juan needed everyone to rest. They'd resume the hunt fresh at daybreak.

One way or the other, Juan would have his prisoners by tomorrow. This time, he'd make sure they weren't left unguarded. He'd also strip-search them for tracking devices, since he couldn't fathom how this American woman could have found the man she'd rescued—if they even were traveling together, which he still didn't have official confirmation of.

Juan brought his cross pendant to his lips and kissed the gold crucifix. Tonight, he'd pray to the patron Saint Rose of Lima. She'd understand his need. Rose had dedicated her life to helping her community—just as Juan was trying to do for his own.

The sale of drugs, the kidnappings, and the extortion were merely a means to an end. Life had become so much more complicated since Rose's era. Selling needlework and flowers, like she'd done, wasn't going to cut it in the 21st century.

But if all proceeded as planned, Juan would soon have his captives. Then, he could squeeze them financially dry, and let the jungle finish them off.

He needed the ransom money and hoped to take them alive. Of course, if the photographer and the physician died trying to escape, his organization could simply use that as an example of what happened to capitalist pigs when they came to Colombia.

Eight

G race woke to the rowdy squawking of Capuchin monkeys clinging to a nearby tree. She started to stir, but froze when she felt a muscular body resting beside her. She'd been so deeply asleep that she'd forgotten she wasn't alone.

Lying beside her in the hammock, Wade smelled like the little bottle of citrus soap she'd brought with her but mixed with his own scent of sage. She turned her head to look at him. In the dim morning light, the dark whiskers of his square jawline were visible. She smiled at the sight of his wavy hair gone wild in his sleep.

Lips curled at the edges, Grace began to move her hand off his firm abdomen.

At her movement, Wade stirred. He turned slightly in the hammock and tightened his hold on her. Grace's body responded to his heat and touch, flooding her with a warm sensation in her core that made her heart beat faster.

She stiffened before reassuring herself this was probably an entirely normal physiological response. After all, she hadn't slept—in any sense of the word—with a man in two years.

"Wade?"

When he wriggled against her, she bit back a groan.

"*Wade*?"

His eyes flickered open. She gave him a moment to remember that he was in a jungle, sleeping with a stranger, in a hammock swinging twelve feet above the ground.

When his dark blue eyes finally blinked with registration, Wade grinned rather than letting her go. His eyes lit with desire.

Swallowing back her physical response, she tried not to think about how their bodies were separated by nothing more than a couple of layers of thin clothing.

"I need your help getting out of the hammock," she said.

"Sure. What can I do?" He moved his hands down to her waist as she sat up.

"There's no graceful way to do this," she warned, "and I need to pee. So, put your hands wherever you need to in order to hoist me out while keeping me from falling back on top of you."

"That doesn't sound too difficult."

When Grace shot him a look over her shoulder, he chuckled.

As Wade hoisted her up, she reached outside the mosquito net for one of the dangling ropes. At the same time, she extended a foot across to a nearby branch.

When the swing of the hammock started to pull her away from the tree, Wade gave her a firm push on the buttocks, launching her across the gaping chasm until she was safely standing on the thick limb.

"That was *not* intentional," Wade called out to her, holding out the hands he'd cupped her backside with.

She laughed. The touch had been brief and accidental, but her heartbeat punched upward like she'd been shocked. "It's okay. I needed the boost." She smiled as she slipped into the harness.

Seemingly encouraged by her reaction, he grinned. "Full disclosure, though, I might have enjoyed it."

She arched an eyebrow at him and attempted to suppress a grin as he smiled wryly at her. Feeling his eyes on her, Grace lowered herself from the tree.

"I think you enjoyed it, too," he called after her as she descended.

She didn't look up, but she felt warmth spread up her neck and into her cheeks and ears.

CONSTANCE WATCHED THE EXCHANGE, rubbing her hands together with greedy delight. Her plan seemed to be working after all, and fortunately the weather was cooperative.

In addition to her ability to see into the future, if Constance focused properly, she could also stir a little wind, move a few clouds or fog, and even disrupt electrical currents. All were very minor except in rare circumstances.

Although she'd had nothing to do with the rain and mudslide, the such romantic detour was a delightful bonus. Now, more urgent matters took precedence. The cute couple still needed to make it to the airstrip to escape this jungle.

Airstrip. Ha! Some might be more inclined to call a strip of pasture land, and it was still a fair distance away.

Back up in the tree, Grace and Wade worked together to untie the ropes, hammock, and tent. After they'd untied everything, the two of them descended the tree, one at a time, using the harness and ropes.

Constance enjoyed watching them work together. She hadn't yet informed Grace that the hunt for Wade Rawlings was well underway. Their initial search had taken the guerrillas down Grace's decoy path, which had given Grace and Wade a good head start—until the mudslide.

Now, the pair were behind schedule. And this morning, the Colombians were broadening their search and strategically including every means of extrication from the jungle, including the local airstrips.

Grace needed to arrive at the rendezvous point on time and use her green smoke flare to signal the pilot that he was safe to land his tiny, single-engine casket—er, *plane*—to extract them. If he didn't see the smoke signal at the agreed upon time, the pilot had been ordered to circle the landing strip just once before leaving.

If he left, Grace and Wade were as a good as dead. Without a plane, there'd be no leaving the Colombian jungle, and they wouldn't be able to outrun the guerrillas for long.

Constance fanned herself with her hands as she floated toward Grace.

"You two need to get a move on."

"Trouble?" Grace raised an eyebrow as she rolled up the hammock. Across the clearing, Wade rolled up the tent.

"I'm worried the Colombians will reach the airstrip before you do," Constance explained.

"Well, will they?"

Constance drew her lips in a straight line. "I can't tell." She couldn't see *everything*.

"Okay—we'll move faster."

"What trouble?" Wade asked.

Constance noted he didn't seem unduly perturbed about Grace communicating with an entity he could neither see nor hear.

Grace turned to him. "Constance says your captors are advancing on our airstrip. It's going to be a race to the finish line."

She began packing supplies faster as she spoke, fashioning the harness into a back strap and securing the tent, blanket, and hammock to it. She deftly secured the equipment. Constance had been with Grace on her many hiking trips—some peaceful, domestic excursions and others with danger hot on her heels. The dangerous ones had only been in the last few years—ever since Daniel's death. Each had been more dangerous than the last, and each had required increasingly faster packing skills.

Well, if Grace was determined to tempt fate—perhaps to join Daniel sooner than destiny had intended—Constance could at least try to counter that by using her powers of perception to keep Grace alive; and hopefully rediscover her passion for life.

Wade finished packing the backpack and slung it over his shoulders. "We good?"

Grace nodded, cinching the harness. "Ready."

Constance took the lead, and the three of them began the trek.

WADE KEPT up with the brisk pace set by Grace. As he hiked, he thought about what a weird trio they made: A photographer, a physician, and an imaginary ghost dodging armed guerrilla fighters. There were worse ways to spend the night in a jungle than holding a competent and beautiful woman, but the impending threat of their pursuers kept him from truly enjoying the moment.

This wasn't Wade's first brush with danger. He'd been on a chopper from Kabul to Ghanzi—photographing the ravages of war—when enemy fire riddled the chopper. The helicopter had been forced to land in Taliban-controlled territory, and for two days Wade snuck through hazardous mountains and arid desert to reach safety.

At least the jungles of Colombia were prettier.

He tried to quell his nagging worry over the dwindling probability of escape by staying observant of his surroundings. "I wish I had my camera," he lamented. "The exotic plants and wildlife are breathtaking."

"Maybe you can come back after this and take more pictures of the Amazon. Just take a different route back home next time." Grace held a cluster of vines aside for Wade to walk past.

"My equipment's gone." He sighed. "No photos means no payment—and no payment means no way to buy replacement equipment."

They trudged through the jungle in silence. He hoped his complaint hadn't sounded like an invitation for her to offer to buy him new equipment. He'd figure something out when he got home.

Eventually, Grace broke the silence. "I'm sorry about your crew. Even if I'd arrived sooner, I don't think I could have done anything for them."

"Please don't apologize. We were in the wrong place at the wrong time. I'm nothing but grateful you arrived when you did."

Grace snorted. "Don't thank me yet."

"I *am* thanking you." He laughed bitterly. "Accept it. Even if they beat us to the plane, you did everything you could." He reached out and touched her arm softly, adding, "So, thank you, Grace."

She turned and smiled. "You're welcome."

As she resumed walking, he followed closely behind and worked up the courage to ask, "When we're back home, maybe I can buy you a drink sometime?"

An inexplicable flutter buzzed in his chest. Did he just ask her on a date?

This woman clearly wasn't even operating with a full deck of cards—not with the whole imaginary ghost friend thing. So, why did he feel nervous about her response? Why was his heart counting the beats as the seconds ebbed by? Grace was an attractive, fit, and intelligent physician—despite the paranormal delusions. She was also apparently rich. Yeah. She was out of his league, and that made him nervous.

"Sure," she answered casually. "We can reminisce about

that time in the Colombian jungle over a glass of Guinness."

"Yeah," Wade chuckled humorlessly. His initial relief that she'd agreed was quickly replaced with confusion. Reminisce? Did she just transform his asking her out into something platonic? He'd have to remedy that.

"Wade."

He stopped suddenly—but not before almost running into her.

She turned to face him, and their bodies were almost touching.

"We're two miles out," she warned, "which means we need silence from here to the airstrip."

He nodded—even though what he really had the urge to do was pull her into his arms and fit their bodies together like they had in the hammock.

Get a grip, Wade.

Normal people didn't make out in a jungle.

Then again, normal people also didn't follow a ghost through the aforementioned jungle, and normal people probably didn't risk their lives photographing the beauty enveloped in danger in that same jungle. Or equally hazardous places elsewhere across the world.

Clearly, there was nothing normal about either of them.

Before he had a chance to do something stupid about it —like lean in for a kiss—Grace resumed walking.

Slow your shutter speed, Wade. Some rich chick with a reckless side doesn't want your cheap hands all over her.

As soon as that thought escaped his mind, he knew it was unfair to Grace. She'd never behaved in any way to suggest she thought herself better than him. Not to mention, out of all the people in the world she could have used her resources to help rescue from danger, she had chosen *him*.

Nine

Grace motioned for Wade to crouch, dropping down to her knees herself. The two of them remained hidden under the cover of the lush jungle ferns, but through the foliage, she could make out the clearing ahead where their landing strip was located.

The Cessna they were trying to rendezvous with was parked at the end of the runway, engine off.

"Dammit." She hissed out the word.

On the other side of the fern, Constance began chewing her translucent nails, staring at the plane. She was clearly as concerned as Grace was.

Wade crouched so close behind Grace that he bumped elbows with her beneath the cover of the ferns. He followed her line of sight.

"I see the plane. What's the problem?" he asked.

Easing the harness off her back, she gave her shoulders a rest. "The pilot wasn't supposed to land—not without my flare signal."

"But he's here now. We have a ride out, right?"

Grace shook her head as a lump formed in her throat. How did she tell Wade she'd failed him?

She rubbed her temple. "If he landed and parked on this strip, that means he's working for the Colombian fighters."

"You're sure that's our plane?"

"I'm sure." Her mind raced. What were their options now?

Turning to her ghostly friend, she said, "Constance, if I try to negotiate with them, will they accept payment and let us go?"

Constance's eyes fluttered as she focused on the future and the outcome if Grace followed a specific course of action.

"I'm not letting you do that," Wade interrupted, but neither Grace nor her ghostly genie listened to him.

"No, Darling," Constance warned Grace. "If they seize you, they'll never let you go. And Wade won't survive."

Grace swallowed and took his hand. "I should have made a backup plan."

Her gaze snagged on movement by the plane. "Wait, I see the pilot. Constance, can you tell what he's saying to the guy with the AK-47?"

The two men were smoking, but she was too far away to hear them—not that she'd be able to understand them, anyway. Her Spanish was still a work in progress and better suited to asking a patient to stick out a tongue than understanding an exchange between two sketchy villains.

Constance accepted the task, though, and vanished.

That left Grace alone with Wade. She looked down at their hands, only now realizing she'd intertwined her fingers with those of the handsome photographer. When she started to pull her hand away, he clasped it with both of his.

"I'm sorry," she said, still staring at their joined hands. "We can keep hiking north until we reach a town, but we'll run out of food in a day."

He cupped her chin and brought it up until they were making eye contact. "You got me out of that pit, Grace. I thought I'd die in there. If you managed that, I know we'll get through this, too—together."

She nodded, staring into those warm blue eyes and full lips framed in stubble.

She was so close to him, kneeling in the ferns, that one small motion would bring her close enough to sink her fingertips into his thick, black hair. The air grew quiet as the leaves faintly danced around them.

"So," Constance's shimmering apparition reappeared in a puff of blue smoke—very genie-like.

Startled, Grace pulled back from Wade and released his hand. "Constance!"

"Oh, damn." Constance looked back and forth between the two of them with a wry smile. "I interrupted something, didn't I? Was there magic in the air? Were you going to kiss him, you saucy vixen?"

"*No!* Knock it off. What did you hear?"

"They're contemplating why you're late. One of them suggested checking the river, so two men are hiking down there while the other two stay here. Two more are retracing their steps back to camp."

Grace relayed everything to Wade.

"Two here." His brows furrowed. "I'm not sure we can take two armed men."

"Even if we could—then what? I can't fly a plane."

"I can," he shrugged. "I mean, I'm not a pilot yet, but I've logged forty hours of flight time—and another forty on the simulator."

She stared at him, wanting to kiss him even more this time.

He shrugged, his cheeks turning red. "I did so much remote travel and learned a lot from pilots over the years, I decided to work toward getting my recreational pilot certificate. Single-engine planes I can do. Helicopters? I'm not so good at them yet."

"Okay." Grace beamed. "We have a pilot."

"I can take out the two men," Constance said.

Grace turned to her, astonished. "How?"

"You know I was responsible for the plague of locusts in Capua in 203 B.C.?" She paused. "Well, not *directly* responsible—the swarm was coming anyway. My jinn 'magic' merely directed it where it should go."

Grace stared. "Constance, this isn't the time for your ancient war stories."

"Darling, everything is the time for my ancient war stories."

Grace growled in frustration when she wanted to snarl. "You're going to distract them with bugs?"

"Something like that. Move closer to the plane, and on my signal, get to it and take off."

"Oh-kay." Grace's voice dripped with skepticism. "We need a long enough distraction for us to start the plane *and* take off."

"Darling, I never underdeliver."

Grace exhaled—whether from relief or rising fear, she

wasn't sure. She turned to Wade and held up her index finger. "One moment. I'll be right back."

As she walked several steps away from him, Constance followed.

She turned to the genie as she hovered alongside her in a cloud of blue smoke.

"Listen," she told Constance, "I appreciate that you feel like you have to fix everything, but when my wishes went south, it was on me."

Setting a fast pace, Grace tried to piece together her thoughts into something cohesive, but not hurtful. "Your abilities have limits, Constance," she warned. "I'm not faulting you for that. I'm the imbecile that jumped out of a plane over Colombia." She clasped her hands together. "What I'm trying to say is: You could make things worse than they already are."

Constance scowled.

Grace kept on, ignoring the disapproving glare. "Maybe Wade and I should just give the Colombians a wide birth," she suggested. "We could hike north toward Bogotá." She glanced over her shoulder, back at Wade, who stared intently at the ground as though diamonds were buried there. As though sensing her, he perked up and looked her direction.

Constance's reaction wasn't quite so copacetic. "Make things *worse*?" Constance glowered, rising to her full, rather masculine height.

Grace cringed—not out of fear, but out of recognition that she'd just deeply upset her ghostly friend.

"Is that what I do?" Constance boomed. "I make things *worse*?"

"Now, hang on." Grace's defensive temper flared, but she kept her voice a harsh whisper to avoid giving their presence away to the two nearby armed Colombians.

Constance could roar at the top of a mountain—only Grace would hear her. Grace herself, though, couldn't risk speaking too loudly.

"I don't *blame* you," Grace whispered heatedly. "I'm merely suggesting that *sometimes* things don't turn out the way you predicted they would—and we *need* this escape to be a successful one—our lives depend on it."

Constance scoffed. "*All* of my predictions—my guiding your future—have been spot on. You wanted love? I gave you love. You wanted money? I provided it."

She rolled her heavily lashed eyes. "I *never* underdeliver, Darling? Tiglath-Pileser, King of Assyria, wanted a professional army, and I delivered. The maharaja, Shivaji Bhonsle wanted an empire, and yup, I provided that, too." Her face hardened. "Whatever disaster ensued from some cascade of events later down the line—love lost, lives lost, famine, plagues, pestilence ... well, they're your own damn faults!"

Grace clenched her fists. "*Thank you*, Constance." She seethed through gritted teeth. "I'm *well* aware my choices are my own, and that they've ultimately led me to this moment." Grace blinked away angry tears. "Money without love. Possible captivity without end." She turned away, unable to look at Constance anymore.

If Constance was remorseful, she didn't show it. Instead, she seethed. "Oh, don't worry. I'll get you out of this mess—and *then* you won't have to worry about my *interference* anymore."

With that, Constance abruptly vanished.

~

GRACE SAT DEJECTEDLY on an exposed rock with a view of the plane right on the meager runway, waiting impatiently for Constance's signal. Her stomach rolled, but only part of that was from nerves. Most was feeling like she'd ruined her friendship with Constance.

Whatever Constance's distraction turned out to be, she and Wade would have to make a mad dash for the plane as soon as it started. Grace needed to stay alert; she couldn't afford to be off her game.

Wade sat beside her, keeping his voice low. "They might shoot at us," he warned.

"Yeah, they might." Grace nodded. "But only until we're near the plane. I don't think they'd risk firing at it." She twisted her hands together. She'd never been shot at, which she assumed was the reason Wade had mentioned it; to mentally prepare her.

She'd been near weapons in perilous situations, when delivering medical care. Although danger had been present on several of her adventures, she'd never been the specific target of bullets zipping around her and she wasn't all that keen on starting now.

"Have *you* been shot at before?" Grace asked Wade.

He sat beside her on the small rock and took her hands in his. "I've been in war zones before—where bullets and bombs were real threats—but I've only been directly shot at once." He shifted on the rock. "We were taking aerial photos in Afghanistan, and insurgents shot down our helicopter. It was rough, but I survived with the help of the soldiers I was with. Until I got thrown into

GRACELYNN'S GENIE

that pit, that helicopter landing was the most terrified I'd ever been."

Wade then turned to face her, leaning in to cup Grace's chin with his warm, calloused hand.

"If they fire," he murmured, looking deep into her eyes, "just keep your focus on the objective—get to the plane. No matter what, get to the plane. I'll be right by your side."

She looked into his soft, azure eyes—and, for a moment, she felt transported to a shore, as if gazing staring at a tranquil ocean.

His hand on her chin slipped around to the back of her neck.

She smiled weakly. "So much for my grand rescue."

"You came for me, Grace. You risked your life to traipse through the jungle and pull me out of that pit. I don't care that it was some bizarre third wish from a spirit only you can see and hear. You came for me. And I'm damn grateful you did."

Leaning in, she closed the gap between her mouth and his succulent lips. Finally, he kissed her, and as their lips met, she fully accepted his mouth against hers, feeling his firm fingers pressed into her scalp, holding her in place as he deepened the kiss.

She felt transformed in that moment—as if she wasn't in the Colombian jungle at all, but on a secluded romantic getaway with a charming and handsome man.

Who, *oh boy*, knew how to kiss!

When they finally broke away, he smiled at her with a look of sweet intoxication on his face.

"*Gringos! Eschúchame! Levanta tus manos!*"

Grace's blood turned from liquid, steamy lava to frigid

71

ice so fast, it felt like it congealed in her veins. Spinning around, she found herself staring down the barrel of an AK-47 as two Colombian guerrilla fighters, dressed head-to-toe in camouflage clothing, glared murderously at her and Wade.

"*Levanta tus manos!*"

"Okay, okay." Wade slowly raised his hands.

Grace followed suit—glancing around desperately for Constance. The men had snuck up on them so quietly that neither she nor Wade had heard a thing—and Grace hadn't gotten any warning from her spirit friend. She could only hope that meant Constance was preoccupied scheming her plan and hadn't just abandoned them.

Ten

Constance absorbed her surroundings. Somewhere deep in the interconnected, biological machinery of the jungle—from a raindrop, to a ruffle of branches as a red-tailed squirrel leaped from tree to tree, to the fall of a petal on the dirt floor—lay the specific path to enact her plan.

If a butterfly flaps its wings in the Caribbean, does it lead to a typhoon in Japan three weeks later?

Constance wasn't sure about the Chaos Theory, but she was intimately familiar with cause and effect. She didn't have three weeks to wait, though, so she needed more than an airborne butterfly.

Constance clicked her long fingernails together, closing her eyes to focus.

Cause and effect.

When she opened her eyes again, the infinite possibilities fanned out before her in luminous colors—millions of threads linking countless actions and reactions.

Wajadtuha!

She found the one path she needed.

Constance floated toward an arrangement of rocks cascading with dripping water. Using the full force of her supernatural powers, she shoved aside the trickle of water to the left.

A small spray spurted off-course—and, in response, a mosquito that had been flying toward the rocks veered sharply right, sending it into the path of a spotted frog. The frog's black eyes tracked the sudden, unexpected appearance of the mosquito before instinctively lashing out it's tongue.

The quick motion caused the broad leaf the frog was perched on to ripple. That ripple shook a nearby spider web, causing an adjacent assassin bug to leap away from the sticky threads. A small lime and blue tanager, flying past at that exact second, caught the assassin bug in its beak before swooping higher.

The bird flew past hundreds of brown moths, all converged on a tree. The moths were startled, and instantly took flight at the appearance of the fast-moving predator. Like a great, brown cloud of smoke, they flowed toward the airstrip—a fluttering undulation of umber-colored, flapping wings.

While all of that was occurring, Constance took similar action within a small, nearby cave—setting a flock of bats bursting from the darkness toward the airstrip. Their course would not-so-coincidently intersect with the moths.

"*Vamos!*"

Wade scolded himself as he and Grace were marched at gunpoint through the jungle. He'd been passionately kissing Grace when he *should* have been tuned to danger and checking his surroundings.

Wrong as it may sound, there were worse times to die than after a kiss like that. Only, he didn't want to die—and he certainly didn't want to go back into the pit, either. He wanted was more of Grace—talking, and kissing, though preferably not in the jungle or staring down the barrel of a rifle.

He promised himself he'd listen to every whimsical ghost story she had to tell if only they could somehow survive this together.

But even as he thought that, he grudgingly admitted that the evidence of her invisible, intangible genie spirit was becoming harder to dismiss. Wade had no plausible, non-paranormal explanation for how Grace had found him in the first place—not to mention how, after becoming utterly lost during the mudslide, Grace had still managed to find the airstrip, despite not having a GPS or map.

The two of them had been waiting on that rock to see what type of supernatural distraction this so-called Constance would conjure. Wade now promised himself that if this genie actually got them out of their current predicament, he'd be transformed from cynical skeptic to wholehearted believer.

For now, though, he needed to think of a plan that didn't involve either him or Grace getting shot.

The jungle thugs led them at gunpoint through thick, prickly branches and into a clearing. Before them stretched the airstrip—at the end of which squatted the white and blue, single engine Cessna 172 Skyhawk that Grace had been planning for them to escape aboard. It was a 1970s model, Wade guessed, probably plaid interior.

"*Mira lo que he encontrado,*" one of the gunmen said as they approached the plane. A tall Colombian man, who carried himself like the leader of the group, turned to acknowledge the words. He'd been talking and smoking with the pilot, confirming Grace's theory that the pilot had betrayed them.

As they approached the plane, Wade recognized a small pile of boxes and bags on the ground—all of his camera equipment!

After the pilot and the leader of the Colombian rebels exchanged more words and a firm handshake, the pilot began to load Wade's equipment onto his plane.

An exchange. Wade understood now.

The leader stomped out his cigarette underfoot, before turning to glare at Grace and Wade. His dark, greedy eyes examined Grace from head to toe—and when he finally spoke to them, it was in heavily accented English.

"American," he sneered. "Rich, white American. Do you have a daddy who will pay for you? *Me pregunto.*"

Grace stood straight and still as a board.

"You look good enough," the man purred menacingly. "Someone will pay, yes?" He reached up and rubbed strands of her blonde hair between two fingers.

"Keep me," Wade snapped. "Let her go."

The Colombian's eyes flashed, and his nostrils flared. He turned and struck Wade's stomach with a lightning-fast punch. Pain and nausea rocketed through his abdomen as he doubled over. The blow would have been bad enough, but combined with his broken ribs, it was agony.

Throughout it all, Grace never moved.

Instead, she turned to the menacing man and looked deep into his murky brown eyes. Despite being his prisoner —despite having two men with guns behind her—Grace's voice was filled with a dark, terrifying confidence.

"Do you have ghosts from your past Juan Landa?" she asked. Then, eyes narrowing, Grace answered her own question. "Yes, you do, don't you? And they're coming for you, Juan. They're coming for you right now." She uttered her threat in a low, coolly even tone.

Juan seemed to falter at Grace's use of his name, and Wade couldn't blame him. The way Grace spoke—the preciseness of her tone—filled even Wade with ominous dread; as if she relayed things no living being could possibly know.

JUAN BLINKED AT THE AMERICAN—WHO, until a moment ago, he'd considered to be his walking, talking, blonde-haired payday.

What ghosts was she referring to? And how did she know his name?

Something in the woman's chill tone sent icy talons sinking into his chest, squeezing his heart. Instinctively, he reached for the gold cross hanging around his neck.

A Brazilian woman he'd once kidnapped had been similarly—eerily—calm when he'd captured her; reciting a curse against Juan in almost exactly the same tone of voice as this blonde American. That woman had made all his men worry about 'spirits' and similar supernatural nonsense throughout the weeks she'd spent shackled in the camp—until Juan himself had grown unsettled. It was during that Brazilian woman's captivity that he'd begun wearing the gold cross still dangling around his neck.

That had been five years ago, and the medallion had apparently served its purpose in protecting him. Juan was confident it would continue to do so now.

But even as he calmed himself, he heard a strange rustling noise from the thick jungle surrounding them. The noise grew ever louder, as something approached them from the depths of the thick foliage.

Behind him, Juan's men turned from the Americans and leveled their weapons at the edge of the jungle, looking both confused and disconcerted by the rustling hum, which seemed to be reaching a crescendo.

Hundreds—no, *thousands*—of brown and grey moths burst from the forest and flooded the clearing. Like a great, fluttering storm cloud, the solid wall of insects swept directly toward them. Juan staggered back as they over-whelmed him, desperately swatting the moths away from his face, hair, and neck. The thick blanket of frenzied, thrashing wings engulfed him—sending him into panic and confusion.

His men were similarly frightened, flailing uselessly at the insects until their nerves cracked and they cried out, ducking and running for the cover of the jungle.

The pilot, meanwhile—who'd been picking up the last of the American's camera equipment—clutched the bag to his chest and ran desperately for the plane in a haphazard zigzag.

This is absurd!

Even as Juan's heart pounded in his chest, he convinced himself that this rogue swarm of insects would pass momentarily—if everyone just kept their wits about them.

The chaos escalated as a hundred bats swooped from the sky, seemingly from nowhere. The swarm of bats speared through the cloud of moths, devouring them and sending the hysterical storm of insects into even more dizzying circles.

Juan's men ran deeper into the jungle, shrieking. He wheeled around as the cloud of insects began to dissipate, but he didn't see his captives anywhere. They'd vanished in the confusion, like ghosts; or as if they'd been transformed into moths themselves.

For a moment, Juan stood firm—and then, heart threatening to burst, the guerrilla leader followed his men into the jungle; fleeing the unnatural swarms of insects and flapping bats.

Eleven

~~~~~~

Grace darted across the clearing with Wade, heading to the plane and dodging the battle royale being fought all around them by the swarm of moths and bats. As she ran, a rippling blue form shimmered into coalescence alongside her.

"Thank you," Grace panted at the familiar spirit now gliding along beside her.

"It's nice to know I still have my mojo," Constance answered, looking pleased with herself.

That she had—but how had Constance managed such a feat? Well, Grace had heard the genie claim to have turned the tide for great rulers once upon a time, when she'd been the formidable jinn Constantine. She'd also learned, much to Constance's chagrin, that as a ghost, she'd never been written into the textbooks or recognized for the pivotal role she'd played.

Grace recognized that role now, since Constance's distraction had let her and Wade reach the other side of the clearing, and the plane. The door of the Cessna hung open, abandoned by the pilot midway through loading his loot.

Wade hoisted Grace into the small plane. When she turned back to offer her hand and pull him in after her, she caught site of the pilot coming into view, running desperately toward the plane.

"Look out!" Grace cried.

Wade spun, dodging the pilot's fist as he launched himself at the pilot, swinging his own punch in retaliation, which landed solidly on the pilot's jaw. The Colombian stumbled backward, and then Wade was on him with another two punches. After the second blow, the pilot crumpled to the ground and stayed there.

Wade turned and hauled himself inside the plane. Grace yanked the door shut as he slithered out of the straps of the backpack and squeezed himself into the pilot's seat.

She wanted to ask him where he'd learned to fight, but she suspected he'd acquired those skills during his days on photo shoots with soldiers in active war zones.

Behind the yoke, he flipped levers and checked gauges. Grace quietly took off her harness and climbed into the co-pilot's chair, careful not to disrupt Wade's concentration.

Constance shimmered into being and stuck her head between the seats.

"I took care of the distraction," she purred. "The rest is now up to your man, Wade. Bats and bugs are one thing, but airborne contraptions are beyond my scope."

Grace bit her lip and nodded.

Wade had told her he could fly, and she trusted him. He'd had faith that a spirit genie would send them a signal, so Grace owed him faith that he could fly them to safety—

under threat of captivity from the armed men twenty feet away, in a plane the size of postage stamp, and on an airstrip the size of a stick of gum.

Grace looked at Constance and mouthed the words: "I believe in him."

WADE STARED down the nose of a plane at the runway—which was unlike any other he'd ever seen: Narrow, grassy, and short.

The plane had already been lined up on the runway, since the pilot had clearly been intending his takeoff. There'd be no preflight planning, because they had to liftoff before their moment of distraction passed. Instead, Wade did a quick gauge check—just the essentials. The oil pressure and oil temperature were both in the green.

Bumpy landscape aside, there was no crosswind, which meant one less thing to worry about. However, the warm, heavy air would make it harder to takeoff. At least they were several thousand feet above sea level, so the air density wasn't as bad as it could have been in this tropical climate.

He took a shaky breath. As he advanced the throttle, the engine revved faster and louder.

Because of the short-field takeoff, he held down the brake while applying full power to the prop. He'd set the flaps to one notch to give him maximal lift with minimal drag. While he knew the concept behind a short-field take-off, he'd never actually performed one except in simulations.

As he released the brake, the plane launched forward. A

second later, he glimpsed the airspeed indicator, reading thirty-five knots and rising.

The plane's tires bumped and skipped across the rough terrain. He kept a firm grip on the yoke even as his palms began sweating. As their speed increased, he began to pull back on the yoke—slowly adding pressure as the plane reached fifty-five knots indicated airspeed.

The tree line approached so rapidly that his gut clenched. Sweat broke out down his neck and his heart beat faster—driven by the fear that he might not be able to lift them into the air in time. Even if the wheels left the grass, the nose of the plane could still clip the treetops and hurl the little Cessna back into the jungle.

When he felt the aircraft lifting into the air, he glanced over and saw Grace in the corner of his eye. She pursed her lips tightly, a white-knuckled grip on her pant legs.

Wade pulled the yoke back, and they miraculously cleared the treetops. As they rose higher above the jungle, he lowered the nose of the Cessna and raised the flaps—continuing their ascent more gradually.

"You did it!" Grace leaned over and planted a kiss on his cheek.

Step One complete, Wade grinned.

Now, they just had to fly this forty-year-old plane back to Bogotá—and find out how many laws he'd be breaking by attempting an unregistered landing in a major airport. His ears began to pop, and he leveled out. He'd wanted to climb higher for a smoother ride, but the elevation was already five or six-thousand feet alongside the mountain range. He couldn't go above twelve-thousand feet without oxygen—so bumpy ride it would be.

Gripping the shuddering yoke, he looked over at Grace. "Okay, co-pilot," he ordered, "open up that sectional chart, and let's see if we can figure out precisely where we are over Colombia." If he'd had his phone on him, he could have looked up the terrain view for landmarks, but they'd have to make do with a paper map.

Grace beamed at him, looking cute with the bulky headset she'd fitted over her ears and those thick, blonde bangs touching her eyelashes.

She opened the sectional chart, and they talked through where they'd taken off, identifying landmarks and towns as they flew over them. Wade needed to know the names of the landmarks beneath them in order to accurately describe where he was to Colombian air traffic control.

When they were about twenty miles outside of Bogotá, Wade scanned the cabin. Looking to the pilot's side, he found a worn, yellow piece of paper taped to the bulkhead with the radio frequencies for Colombian airports listed on it.

He first squawked 7700 on the transponder, letting air traffic control know he had an emergency. Then, he tried to remember the sequence for an urgent call. Mayday was for loss of aircraft control or a fire—neither of which they were experiencing—but pan-pan would alert ATC to an urgent issue.

He switched the radio to 119.5 for Bogotá approach. "Pan-pan. Bogotá approach. Cessna two-six-zero-five."

"Cessna two-six-zero-five, this is Bogotá approach." The accent was thick, but Wade felt grateful the global language of air traffic controllers was English.

"Cessna two-six-zero-five. Cessna one-seventy-two, south over Chipque at ten thousand MSL."

"Cessna two-six-zero-five. Proceed Parque Metropolitan Simón Bolívar, maintain ten thousand. Expect right traffic runway five."

Wade glanced at the sectional chart that Grace had spread out for him, taking note of the layout of Bogotá. The park named for *El Libertador* Simón Bolívar would be a good landmark for him to follow. He'd be able to spot the large lake there as they flew over the city.

"Cessna two-six-zero-five. Contact El Dorado tower one-one-eight point two-five."

Wade went through the motions of switching frequencies to 118.25 and contacting the tower. He repeated the pan-pan call, and the tower controller directed him to an open runway.

Grace remained quiet and observant throughout all this, which enabled Wade to fully concentrate on flying and landing.

The landing was a little bumpy, but they stayed in one piece as the wheels of the Cessna made contact with the tarmac. Once safely on the ground, Wade taxied the Cessna as instructed by ground control—to where two white and green police cars awaited them.

As his shoulders relaxed in relief, he couldn't help but feel like they'd jumped out of the fire and into the frying pan.

Twelve

Grace sat in the interrogation room feeling stiff and tired. She'd relayed her story to the authorities multiple times—obviously omitting Constance's role.

Her ghostly friend had disappeared during the flight and hadn't yet returned. Perhaps she wasn't going to.

Was this the end? Three wishes had been granted, so perhaps now her genie had vanished, never to reappear.

If that was the case, Grace would have quite the adjustment to make. She'd become accustomed to seeing Constance's translucent form—adorned in blue eyeshadow and wearing blue harem-pants—at least once a week for the last ten years.

They'd been friends who'd parted on bad terms—which sucked.

Grace thought of the lamp that remained in her backpack. The Colombian police had seized her backpack on the tarmac when they'd hauled her and Wade in for questioning. Would she even get it back? The radius of the genie's presence spanned a good fifty miles, but Constance was still intangibly bound to that tangible object.

And what of Wade? Was he being questioned somewhere, too? Were authorities comparing her stories to his, to see if they lined up? Grace and Wade would both describe events that mostly aligned—at least once they'd met up with each other. The exception, though, was why she'd come to Colombia in the first place. Grace had given a rather poor explanation to the police—something about seeking adventure and just happening upon Wade. Perhaps he'd be vague about that part as well. He'd have to be, given how coincidental it all sounded.

Except, there was nothing coincidental in their meeting. Constance had foreseen it all.

Had she foreseen their kiss in the jungle, too?

One tentative night in a hammock and one tentative— yet succulent—kiss, a relationship did not make. Both moments were so brief, so hesitant, and so applicable to a single moment in time that surely they promised nothing more.

Grace couldn't fault Wade if he wanted to distance himself from her—an apparently eccentric millionaire who talked to a ghost.

"That's a glum look for someone who survived the jungle."

Grace lifted her head when she heard the familiar voice. Constance reappeared in a haze of blue smoke.

"Constance!" Grace felt relieved, but then she looked nervously around the small room. "Are the cameras on?"

"No."

Grace stood up and stretched. "Thank you for getting us out of the jungle. I'm so sorry I ever doubted you."

She wanted to ask for ideas on how to get out of the custody of the Colombian national police force, where she'd been trapped for several hours. However, she knew she'd used all three of her wishes. Had she used up her friendship, too?

"In about five minutes, you'll be released with all of your belongings." Constance's tone was full of boastful smugness.

"Oh?" Grace raised an eyebrow. "How'd you manage that?"

"It turns out the Mayor of Bogotá can see ghosts, too. It took me over two hours to find someone in the government hierarchy with the gift. I tried the Operate Directorate of the police first, then two military generals, a brigadier general, a captain, the President, and a special forces commando to no avail. Anyway, I might have invoked the fear of wrathful spirits to do it, but I convinced the Mayor to expedite your release. Of course, he had to speak with the police and confirm your background check first."

"Wow. What about Wade?"

"He'll be released as well—especially since I implied you two were a couple."

"Oh-kay."

"Oh, and I *might* have also promised you'd take the Mayor and his niece to a Yankees game next time he's visiting her. She's studying at NYU." Constance widened her thickly lashed eyes. "I suggest you splurge for the Legend Seats."

"I'll be sure to do that."

The spirit's form rippled and started to grow more and more transparent. She was fading away.

"Wait!" Grace called before the genie vanished entirely. "Are you and I okay?"

Constance smiled and waved a dismissive hand. "Of course, Darling. Life's too short to waste time in a state of anger."

Grace gulped. "Is this goodbye? Will I see you again?"

"Is that a wish?" Constance waggled her eyebrows. "Because I hate to remind you, but you're out of wishes."

"It's me," Grace replied, blinking her glistening eyes, "just wanting to see my friend again."

"Well," Constance sniffed, "I suppose I have forever to find my next victim—er, *wish-maker*—but *you* only have a finite time with *me*; what with how short life is, and all." Her lips curled. "I imagine I could *grace* you with my presence a little while longer."

JUAN'S TEMPER burned through him like a hot flare. So hot, he wondered if smoke was swirling from his ears—the same way it swirled from the cigarette clenched between his fingers.

He drove north on National Route 45 toward Bogotá, replaying the insane events of earlier that day over and over in his mind. A cloud of moths had attracted a flock of bats —all of which had descended on the airstrip; impossibly, *perfectly* timed to allow the Americans to make their getaway.

When Juan had first heard the plane start up and the

engine rev, he'd thought Sal—the pilot—had decided to leave, having delivered the gringos as promised and taken his loot as payment.

But as the insects—and the swooping predators pursuing them—had finally dissipated, he'd watched the plane accelerate down the runway and noticed Sal lying on the ground.

"I can't believe they stole my plane, *hombre*."

Now, that same pilot sat in the passenger seat of Juan's Jeep, running his mouth. Juan wanted to slap the man. He certainly wasn't Sal's *hombre*.

"And that crap on the airstrip? *Loco*, man. *Lo-co*. It felt like an act of God." Sal performed the sign of the cross over his chest.

Juan frowned, taking another drag from his cigarette. God hadn't interfered with his plans—but something had. Spirits perhaps? Old curses?

Regardless of whatever supernatural events were working in the couple's favor, Juan couldn't afford to let those Americans get away. They were his payday.

"I just want my plane back," Sal continued. "I wonder if it's been impounded, or something like that—after an unauthorized landing of an unregistered flight to Bogotá."

Fortunately, Juan had contacts in the *Policía Nacional de Colombia*. He learned that the Americans—Gracelynn Kowalski and Wade Rawlings—had both been taken into custody after landing at the Bogotá airport.

His inside man on the police force would try to stall them as best he could, detaining the Americans until Juan could make it to the city. But Juan was still two hours away, because not only did he no longer have a plane, but he'd had to hump through the jungle to reach his Jeep, followed by spending time finding out where the gringos had gone. Only when he'd got word from his man in the police had he started heading north to Bogotá.

Now, Juan had his foot on the gas and all four wheels on the road, driving fast with two of his best men in the back seat ready to help him reacquire his 'assets.'

Even if that American doctor was released from custody, Juan promised himself that she wouldn't get far. She was a rich white woman in Colombia, and Juan knew her name. She'd have nowhere to hide.

Thirteen

After a warm shower in the comfort of a hotel room, Grace felt incredible. The only thing missing was a night of rest in a real bed—but because her flight home wasn't scheduled until tomorrow, she'd enjoy that final luxury tonight.

Before that indulgence, she needed to meet with the mayor of Bogotá in the hotel restaurant, arranged courtesy of Constance. She adjusted the hem of the dress she'd bought in the hotel lobby, right after checking in. Glancing at the clock, Grace took the opportunity to flop on the couch in her hotel room to relax before she needed to leave.

"Better?" Constance appeared, shimmering into form and hovering above the brass lamp from which Grace had summoned her a decade earlier. After retrieving it from her backpack, Grace had set the lamp on the table so she could stare at it and be reminded of all the enjoyed moments with her genie.

Smoothing the length of her dress, Grace smiled.

"Much better, thank you, but I'll be positively wonderful when I'm stateside."

"And your next trip?"

"I'm not sure." Grace eyed Constance. "I'm a little afraid to ask you for ideas."

"Hmm—as you should be," the genie mused.

"Why? What are you scheming?" Her lips curved.

Constance crossed her arms and changed the subject. "Why'd you run away from Wade?"

Grace lifted her eyes, staring up at the ceiling. "I didn't run away from Wade. I was released from custody before him."

"You could have waited for him. It's like you're determined to unravel all my hard matchmaking."

"I slipped him a note."

"A note? '*Have a safe trip. Look me up if you're ever in New York.*' You call that a note?" Constance scoffed.

"Yes," Grace defended herself. "If he wants to see me again, he can look me up."

"That's the absolute worst invitation in the history of invitations. You might as well have written: '*Thanks for the memories.*'"

Grace, no longer having a restrain herself for fear of discovery by gun-toting guerrillas, raised her voice at the genie. "I don't want him to feel *obligated* to see me just because of everything we've gone through together."

"Because you saved his life?"

"*You* saved his life. I was just the tangible matter to your will."

"*We* saved him."

"Yes, fine—but I don't want an obligatory relationship

93

because *we* saved him." Grace sat up sharply and gently rubbed her temples.

"So, you're hiding from him?"

"I'm not hiding."

Constance sighed—as if she were summoning the strength of a saint to endure this conversation. She picked at her long, azure, sparkling nails before smoothing her fingers over her heavily penciled eyebrows.

"Liar, liar."

"I'm going to dinner." With a huff, Grace slipped on her shoes, snatched up her phone, and retrieved her room keycard. She marched toward the door.

JUAN PARKED his jeep outside the decadent hotel. He'd dropped the pilot off at the airport. During the time it had taken him to drive to Bogotá, he'd had his spies in the city get to work locating which hotel a certain 'Gracelynn Kowalski' had checked into.

He entered the hotel armed with a concealed 9mm Córdova and chloroform. Two of his crew accompanied him. Sneaking his prize out of the hotel would pose a risk—but it was far from impossible. The pretty American doctor was small enough to be folded into the trashcan of a maid's cart. Beyond keeping her alive, the woman's physical wellbeing didn't matter much.

Juan and his men knew which floor Kowalski's room was on and took the elevator upward. When the ding sounded, the three of them exited the elevator and stalked menacingly down the corridor toward her room number. As they approached the door, Juan checked the hallway.

Empty.

One by one, they drew their handguns.

When Juan nodded to the man to his right, he stepped forward and brushed a keycard he'd bribed the corrupt receptionist to create for him against the electronic lock.

They heard a 'click'—and then Juan exploded into the room, gun raised.

"Don't move—or I'll shoot!"

WADE HAD BEEN STANDING outside the hotel room door, debating if he should knock or not, when he'd heard arguing—a one-sided argument.

He smiled. Grace must be arguing with Constance—about *him*, apparently.

Grace had abandoned him back at the police station, leaving nothing but a note. Wade had been determined to find her—if she hadn't left Colombia already.

Working off the assumption that she'd want a shower and a soft bed as much as he did, he figured she'd remain in the city for at least a little while. So, he'd checked into his own hotel room and started calling around, making up stories about looking for his missing friend. Knowing Grace was wealthy, he'd started by calling each of the five-star hotels in Bogotá, asking after a Gracelynn Kowalski. When he'd struck out at the first hotel, he also started asking for anyone who'd checked in with the name of Elvis. At last, one hotel confirmed the presence of a guest called Gracelynn Kowalski—and a different hotel had someone with the name of Elvis.

So, which one was his Grace?

Or what if they both had been reserved by Grace?

Wouldn't a savvy world traveler like her check in under a pseudonym? Would she also pay for a second room somewhere else? Under her real name—just in case she'd thought someone might be after her...

Someone like the leader of a vicious cell of Colombian rebel fighters?

He remembered how Grace had laid a false trail for the guerrillas to follow, back when she'd rescued him from that pit. She was always one step ahead—and with that in mind, he decided to try Elvis's room first.

He arrived at the hotel, and the clerk fortunately bought Wade's story about him being her boyfriend—here to surprise 'Elvis' with flowers.

Yet, once he'd arrived and taken the elevator up to her floor, Wade had hesitated outside Grace's room. What if she didn't want to see him?

Maybe she didn't, but he needed to know one way or another if they had something; or if he'd been nothing but a jungle fling to her.

Then, suddenly, the door had swung open, and a startled Grace stood in the doorway with flushed cheeks. She'd stammered out his name.

Grace's golden hair was brushed straight and down, and she wore a bright, red, floral dress. Standing in the doorway, she'd shot a glare over her shoulder, which Wade suspected was directed at Constance.

"Still have your ghost?" He smiled.

"Yes." Flustered, Grace turned back to him, brushing strands of blonde hair from her face. "And she's still putting on a performance."

"May I come in?"

"Yes, of course." Grace stepped aside.

Wade walked in and Grace let the door close behind him.

"Did you get your equipment back?"

"All of it." Wade nodded.

He handed her the bouquet of flowers he'd brought. After she took them with an astonished 'thank you', he held up the note Grace had left for him. "This doesn't work for me."

She licked her lips and swallowed. "What do you mean?"

"I mean: I don't want to wait until New York to see you again—to kiss you again." He stepped forward, crowding her personal space.

Her eyes widened, but she didn't back away from him. Her hands lowered, moving the bouquet out of the space between them.

Leaning closer, his lips hovered less than an inch from hers. He looked from her lips, up to Grace's emerald-green eyes, and then back to her lips again.

"But, just to be clear," he reassured her, "I'm not doing this out of obligation. You pulled me from the pit, but I flew us to safety. We're even."

"We're even," Grace agreed in a husky tone.

She was the one who finally closed the distance, pressing her lips to his. The sweet, succulent taste of them lit a fire inside his heart. Wrapping his arms around her, he pulled her body flush against his and lost himself in the feel of her curves and taste of her mouth.

After several minutes of kissing, they finally broke apart —both breathless.

"Wow," Grace said, exhaling. "I'd continue this— believe me, I would—but I have dinner reservations." She paused, biting her lip. "Care to join me?"

"I'd like that." Wade looked from his jeans and collared shirt to her dress. "But am I underdressed?"

She linked her arm through his. "You're perfect."

Fourteen

❦

Grace entered the hotel dining room with Wade on one side and Constance on the other. They were led to a table where an older Colombian gentleman sat, wearing an elegant suit and a pleasant smile.

Grace extended her hand. "Mayor Carlos Álvarez—I'm Gracelynn Kowalski and this is my friend Wade Rawlings." She turned. "Wade—this is the man who facilitated our release."

She noted Wade's expression of surprise quickly transformed into a smile as he greeted the Mayor with an enthusiastic handshake.

"I'm grateful—and I'm sorry if we caused any delays at the airport with our unauthorized landing."

Carlos waved a dismissive hand. "I think it's all fun and gossip now. What do the kids say? It went *viral*—which I believe means anyone initially put out by the events is now claiming to have been part of them."

Wade chuckled as he pulled out Grace's chair for her. He sat beside her.

The Mayor continued—but this time he addressed Constance—or, to any bystanders, the empty seat which she now occupied. "You'll be relieved to know your scheme worked. Juan Landa and two of his operatives stormed the hotel room that *señorita* Kowalski had booked under her real name just moments ago. The national police have him in custody."

"Marvelous," Constance crooned.

"That's a relief." Grace extended her arm and laid her fingers over Wade's hand, where it rested on the table.

"So," Wade asked, looking back and forth between the Mayor and Grace. "Do you two know each other?"

"No," Grace explained. "Constance introduced herself to the Mayor and explained our situation. He then facilitated our release."

"Oh—so you can see the genie, too?" Wade asked Carlos.

The Mayor smiled. "Yes—but please, let's not go around spreading rumors that the Mayor of Bogotá can see and hear ghosts."

"I wouldn't dream of it."

The waiter arrived to take their drink orders.

"Honestly, I'd love an ice-cold beer," Grace admitted.

"Then, I'd recommend the Monserrate Red Beer," the Mayor offered. "It's a craft beer made right here in Bogotá."

"Sounds perfect."

"I'll have the same," said Wade.

"Make it three," the Mayor grinned.

As the waiter left with a nod, Grace turned to Wade. "The Mayor is going to come to New York next spring for a

Yankees game. His niece is at NYU." She paused. "Would *you* like to join us for a baseball game?"

Wade brightened. "I'd like that."

"Finally," Constance rolled her thickly lashed eyes. She then turned them toward the Mayor. "Do you have any idea how exhausting it was playing matchmaker to a reluctant bachelorette? She's *finally* embracing the possibility of a future with this man."

Grace pointedly ignored Constance, continuing to speak to Wade despite her hot cheeks.

"My treat," she promised Wade. "Legend Seats."

"*Now* you're trying to chase him off by reminding him you're rich," Constance snorted.

Grace suppressed an eye roll. She was having beers in a private room in a five-star hotel with the Mayor of Bogotá. She didn't need to *remind* Wade she had money and connections.

When the waiter brought them their beers, they each took a long drink.

"A wise man chooses a woman based on all of her strengths," the Mayor commented, licking the foam from his lips.

"I agree." Wade's words came out hesitantly, because he hadn't heard Constance's part of this conversation.

The Mayor stood. "I know I'd planned to dine with *señorita* Kowalski this evening, but I feel I should leave you two to enjoy dinner alone—and this is *my* treat. This way, you'll have some fond memories of my country, rather than only terrifying ones. And perhaps you'll want to return someday."

Wade stood and shook his hand again. "I look forward to seeing you in New York, Mayor Álvarez."

"I as well, *señor* Rawlings. As we say in Colombia—*que tenga una buena noche!*"

As the mayor walked away, Wade turned to Grace. "Dinner?"

"I'd love dinner."

~

~~SIX MONTHS LATER~~

GRACE SAT across the table from Wade after they'd finished eating. Constance had left them undisturbed for the duration of the meal. Wade had cooked homemade lasagna, enjoyed at Grace's dining room.

This had been just one of the many dates they'd enjoyed since returning from Colombia—but she and Wade had also taken three international trips over the past six months. During each of them, Grace had administered much-needed medical care to underserved communities, while Wade had photographed the poverty or conflict in the region.

They'd made a great team, and Constance hadn't needed to help them out of any more dangerous situations.

The Mayor of Bogotá had visited New York as promised, and Grace and Wade had taken him and his niece to the Yankees game—Legend Seats.

Wade had earned his pilot license in the meantime, and Grace had slowly come to feel the closest to fully healed that she'd ever felt since Daniel's death.

Her life with Wade left her feeling fulfilled each and every day.

Wade rose from the table. "Come with me." His blue eyes sparkled. "I have something to show you."

He took her hand and led her down the hallway to one of the many entertainment rooms. He pushed open the doors.

Within, a hammock stretched between two large palm trees; planted in enormous ceramic pots. The darkened room was bathed in electric green light, which slowly panned and rippled across the walls and ceiling as jungle sounds played from a sound system hidden in the darkness.

She laughed. "What is *this*?"

"A walk down memory lane." He grinned. "Our first night together—minus the mosquitos and the threat upon our lives."

"It's fantastic!"

Wade walked toward the hammock, which was secured only a few feet off the ground. "Come—get in with me."

After he'd clambered inside, Grace eased herself in beside him. She curled her body close to his.

"Perfect."

"Almost." He withdrew a small box from his pocket. As the hammock swung gently to and fro, he opened the box to reveal a beautiful, gleaming diamond ring.

"I love you so much, Grace. You've filled my life in amazing ways and made wishes I'd never even known I wanted come true. Grant this one for me: Marry me."

"I will." Blinking away tears, Grace stretched over and kissed him.

~~~CONTINUE READING~~~

IN BOXED SETS

Romancing the Spirit

Individual Books

Romancing the Spirit Series #1
Sadie's Spirit / Willow's Windfall
Cassie's Chase / Phoebe's Pharaoh
Vanessa's Valentine / Autumn's Angel
Romancing the Spirit Series #2
Carol's Christmas / Allison's Alibi
Gracelynn's Genie / Michelle's Miracle
Heather's Hero / Chloe's Cupid
Romancing the Spirit Series #3
Sabrina's Storm / Jenny's Justice
Stella's Star / Gigi's Gift
Phoenix's Phantom / Fiona's Freedom

THE CHRISTMAS COLLECTION

Other Books by CB Samet

Looking for more romantic suspense with more action and sizzle? How about with an urban fantasy twist? Check out my supernatural adventures...

The Shadow Guardians Trilogy

Urban fantasy Norse Mythology Adventure

Get *Raven's Flight, a prequel novella* for FREE. In my newsletter, you'll learn about me, special discounts, and new releases.

Raven's Flight, prequel novella

Raine Down, Book 1

Rosalyn's Run, novella

Storm Surge, Book 2

Anka's Orb, novella

Sky Fall, Book 3

Olympian Awakenings Trilogy

Urban fantasy Greek Mythology Adventure

Grab the prequel exclusively HERE.

Stone Hearts

Winds of Destiny

Flame and Shadow

~

The Rider Files

Romantic Suspense Thrillers

Meridian File / Masters File / Box Set 1

McMillan File / Maltisse File /Box Set 2

Storm File / Sullivan File / Box Set 3

Sharp File / Sizani File / Box Set 4

Rivera File / Rucker File / Box Set 5

Richmond File / Redwood File / Box Set 6

Atlas File / Angel File / Box Set 7

Buy 4book box sets direct from author and save 10%

Payhip. Use code E152M0GZG4

Michelle's Miracle

A medium who guards her heart. A man who's finally picked up the pieces of his own. And the ghost determined to bring them together.

Chapter 1 (excerpt)

Michelle walked for an hour through New York City blocks to get from her apartment in Park Slope to the commercial building for her appointment. The cool spring air chilled her cheeks, but her brisk pace, overcoat, and hat kept her core warm.

When she arrived at her destination, she took the stairs to the fourth floor and walked the corridor to find her new accountant.

She came to the office with the business name on the door:

CONNOR ROSS, CPA

She knocked and slowly entered the office.

A man about her age, mid-thirties, stood and came out from behind his oak desk. "Ms. Barcella, you're very punctual."

The man had dark brown hair and an immaculately trimmed beard just long enough to be a beard rather than stubble. The room and his appearance conveyed professionalism.

She shook the hand he offered as she glanced around the small office appraisingly. The furniture was tasteful—darkly stained wood against light gray walls. A painting of a frosted mountain peak hung on the wall opposite the desk.

"I'm Connor Ross."

"Oh." She dropped her hand. She thought this younger man was the office manager or receptionist. "I was expecting someone older and maybe balding. That's incredibly stereotypical of me."

He shrugged and grinned. "Another twenty or thirty years and you might be right. Although, my father still has a full head of hair, so I've got that in my favor."

He walked around his desk and slipped on a pair of reading glasses. "Are you ready to get started? If you'd like, I can get you a cup of coffee, a soda, or bottled water."

Behind Connor and off to the wall by the window, the faint shimmer of a woman dressed in blue jeans and a pink sweater rippled into view. She stood, staring out the window.

Please, not here ... not today.

Michelle bit back a groan. She just wanted someone to help her with money management—not someone haunted by a ghost. "Maybe this was a bad idea."

"I'm sorry?" Connor's expression turned confused.

"You're obviously busy. I shouldn't take up your time."

"You have an appointment," he reminded her with a bemused expression.

"Right." She glanced at the brunette near the window and back at Connor. Maybe if the woman stayed over there, Michelle could get through this appointment. "It would be rude of me to leave. I'll stay." She handed him her folder containing the documents outlining her assets. She had an electronic version she could send but wanted to meet the person who might manage her accounts before sending personal information.

"Please, have a seat."

He waited patiently as she carefully took off her hat and coat and set them down in the client chair beside her. He settled into his leather chair across from her at the large desk.

The ghost by the window turned her attention to the two of them. Michelle concentrated on not making eye contact with her so the ghost wouldn't know she could see her.

"Oh, Connor," the woman said in a pitying voice. "When a pretty woman like that enters your office, you need to take her coat for her." She sighed. "How are you ever going to remarry?"

Connor, oblivious to the woman's gentle chiding, looked intently over Michelle's documents.

Michelle's gaze fell on a photograph on his desk. The woman, who was now a ghost, looked very alive in the photo as she smiled and pressed one rosy cheek against Connor's cheek. He wore a delighted smile.

"What did you have in mind?" Connor asked.

"Hmm? Oh. I'd like to set up some accounts with the money from my parents' life insurance policy. I was thinking of investing in a variety—bonds, stocks, and real estate. A sum should be safely earning interest that will create a monthly stipend for me. And a certain amount would need to be set aside for retirement."

"Both of your parents passed?" He set down his glasses, looked at her, and folded his arms on his desk.

"Plane crash a year ago. I'm finally getting around to making financial decisions."

"I'm sorry for your loss. I know what it's like to lose a loved one."

"Your wife." Michelle regretted the words the instant they were out of her mouth.

"Um, yes. Leukemia. How did you know?"

"You have a picture of the two of you here, but you're not wearing a wedding ring."

And I can see her spirit by the window, she didn't add.

Michelle had dodged enough questions around the knowledge she inadvertently learned by seeing and talking to ghosts that she could think fast on her feet to provide alternative explanations. Except now, Connor was probably wondering why Michelle was noticing the absence of a wedding ring. At least that was perhaps less creepy than the conclusion people sometimes drew—that she'd cyber-stalked them and learned personal information online.

"I'm sorry," she told him. "What was her name?"

Connor looked at the picture frame on his desk. "Penny." He dropped his head back down, placing his glasses back on, and looked at Michelle's finances.

"Oh, Connor." Penny shook her head sadly. "You've got a gorgeous woman—who checked out your appearance and noted you're single—in your office and you can't even *see* her."

Michelle bristled and pursed her lips tight to avoid the temptation to correct Penny. Michelle was not "checking him out."

Penny continued, talking to her husband even though he couldn't hear her. "She's single," she sing-songed. "Oh! And she's an artist."

Michelle leaned back and crossed her legs. She gave Connor a disarming smile to cover her strange behavior. Ghosts had an irritating ability to glean personal information from people. She wanted to tell Penny that the best thing she could do for her husband was to move on and let him have peace. However, she kept silent because if she spoke to the ghost, her medium abilities would be revealed.

Connor adjusted his glasses. "We can definitely do a retirement account and investments. I'll need to know what your monthly budget is, including recurring payment amounts—house, car, student loans."

"No debt. I can send my monthly expenses to you in an email."

"Okay. I'll pull the paperwork together for you to give me proxy to set these accounts up. We'll arrange a day and time for you to come back and sign them."

Come back?

Perhaps everything could be done from email from now on, enabling Michelle to avoid Penny. She could provide her signature through online applications. Michelle felt bad for the ghost and empathized with Connor's loss, but ghosts had a tendency to fixate on ideas and make themselves a nuisance to those who could see them.

"Yes," Penny cheered. "She'll be back, which means you'll have a second chance to make a first impression."

Michelle shot Penny a glowering look as she reached for her coat and hat. She wasn't some ghost's plaything.

Penny blinked in shock.

Oh, no.

Standing, Michelle tugged her coat off the chair and turned to Connor. She needed to make a fast exit, though she found the man attractive and might have considered staying longer if not for the ghost.

"Okay. Thank you for your time. You have my contact info."

Connor stood when she stood, taking off his glasses and tapping them on his chin as he watched her fumble to pull on her jacket. He stepped forward and held the coat up so she could find the other arm hole.

"Thank you." Slipping it on, she turned to leave, but Connor was standing between her and the door. And he was close, apparently baffled into immobility by her rush to leave.

When she looked up at him, he gave a slight smile. She smiled in return and began to regret needing to make a hasty retreat. He didn't move, as if her presence short-circuited his logic. She wasn't sure she minded.

"You saw me!" Penny declared. "You can hear me!"

Michelle straightened her collar and side-stepped the accountant. After hastily yanking open the door, she walked toward the stairs.

Connor stepped after her into the hall. "I'll email you."

"Sounds perfect." She forced cheer into her voice as she waved without turning around. "Thank you!" she called over her shoulder.

The ghost was hot on her heels. "Wait. I've never been seen by the living. How can you do that?"

Michelle reached the stairwell. "It's a curse."

"It's a miracle!" Penny glided effortlessly beside Michelle as she rushed down the stairs.

"No. It really isn't." Michelle had had some good relationships and had helped other ghosts move on, but some were needy and clingy. She sensed the ghost of a young woman, who lingered to watch her husband's every day activities, was in no frame of mind to consider moving on.

"It's fate," Penny added.

"Not really. You need to move on and stop haunting your husband."

"I just want him to be happy. He needs to find someone."

"Happiness is intrinsic. It doesn't come from a person."

"We all need love," Penny countered.

Michelle stopped abruptly at the bottom of the stairwell and looked at Penny. "Well, I can't argue with that."

Penny smiled sweetly.

Connor stood in his office, trying to remember what was next on his agenda after Ms. Barcella. He tried to recall the last time a beautiful woman around his age was in his office.

Probably not since Penny.

Michelle was beautiful and ... strange. Her expressions varied from congenial to flashes of irritation that didn't seem directed at him. She was obviously distracted, which explained why she hadn't used but a fraction of the one-hour consultation she'd scheduled.

Then his eyes fell on the hat on the floor. It must have fallen when she hurried to stand and don her coat.

He picked it up, walked to the elevator, and took it to the ground floor. Gaze scanning the tiny lobby, he didn't see her. Well, he could give it to her when she came back to sign the papers.

From the stairwell, he heard Michelle's voice. She pushed through the door and startled at Connor's appearance. When she looked up at him, there was that smile again. Confident and genuine.

"Ms. Barcella, you forgot your hat." He extended it to her.

"Thanks. And please, call me Michelle." She took the hat, their fingers brushing for only a moment.

"Michelle," he said dryly, taking a step back, because the proximity and touch did something strange to his body. "Who were you talking to?"

Her smile widened, eyes sparkling. "One of the eccentricities of being an only child and an artist is talking to yourself."

He suddenly felt foolish, rushing after her to return her hat with nothing else to say. "I noticed you didn't take the elevator. You don't like elevators?"

She chuckled. "I was trapped inside an elevator once with a wailing banshee for twenty-three minutes. Never again."

Connor pictured a hysterical woman's claustrophobic anxiety clashing with Michelle's calm demeanor. Still, it seemed an odd reason to avoid elevators. Surely the chances of a strange encounter like that happening twice would be rare.

"What type of art do you do?" He struggled to keep the conversation going, though couldn't say why he wasn't ready to let her leave.

"Acrylic mostly, but I like to sketch with charcoal."

"Wow. And the paintings—are they portraits or landscapes or abstract?"

"Mostly landscapes but I'm adding abstract. I like to recreate the landscape of places I've traveled. However, I haven't traveled much and certainly haven't flown since my parents' death, so I've done less landscaping lately."

"Understandable." Loss of a loved one in a plane crash seemed a plausible way to develop a fear of flying. "Do you have a gallery or display in town?"

"Not yet. Putting your artwork on display is a bit like baring your soul. I'm not ready for that type of exposure."

Connor shifted his weight. "Well, I don't have a critical eye, and I enjoy most art, so I can offer encouraging appraisal with the absence of judgment."

"Are you asking for a private viewing?"

"Um. No. Well, I don't know." He'd been attempting friendly conversation, but he had no idea what a private viewing involved. It sounded far too intimate.

Michelle did that thing again where she glanced to one side as though an irritating fly buzzed nearby.

"Thanks for the hat." She fitted it back over impossibly long strands of dark, silky hair before walking out of the building.

Connor stood there feeling like a fool. He was trying to be friendly, but the interaction had dissolved into ...

something. Or had it escalated to something? He wasn't sure.

Probably best he just let that one go. The few dates he'd had since Penny's death often deteriorated into him talking about his wife and the other women talking about their ex-husbands or ex-boyfriends. Younger women were disappointed by his robust work ethic that didn't include weekend parties, and the older ones were embarking on new or second careers post-divorce and didn't have time for the activities he enjoyed.

With his hands in his pockets, he took the elevator back up to his office. Work was his comfort zone, and wilderness hiking was his passion. Neither required an abundance of interpersonal relationship skills.

"Michelle," he murmured, unsettled and intrigued. "Who are you?"

<<<BUY MICHELLE'S MIRACLE>>>

www.ingramcontent.com/pod-product-compliance
Lightning Source LLC
Chambersburg PA
CBHW021118130626
46554CB00002B/755